THE

CLOUD

A NOVEL

FRANK PALESCANDOLO

iUniverse, Inc.
Bloomington

The Cloud

iUniverse books may be ordered through booksellers or by contacting:

iUniverse
1663 Liberty Drive
Bloomington, IN 47403
www.iuniverse.com
1-800-Authors (1-800-288-4677)

Because of the dynamic nature of the Internet, any web addresses or links contained in this book may have changed since publication and may no longer be valid. The views expressed in this work are solely those of the author and do not necessarily reflect the views of the publisher, and the publisher hereby disclaims any responsibility for them.

Any people depicted in stock imagery provided by Thinkstock are models, and such images are being used for illustrative purposes only.

Certain stock imagery © Thinkstock.

Front Cover Art by Andrea Mantegna

ISBN: 978-1-4697-3573-3 (sc)
ISBN: 978-1-4697-3572-6 (e)

Printed in the United States of America

iUniverse rev. date: 10/29/2012

Contents

*The novel was urged on the author
by the reading of "The Cloud of the Unknowing,"
a mystical treatise of the 14th Century*

The Asteroid

C hristopher Christopherson is longer than his name. He is six foot three, a long tanned face grizzled by high altitude air, frosty fair hair worn lengthy across his broad back, thick alpaca jacket, and leather pants. He was sitting at his desk at the open window with a view of the observatory on the peak of this mountain in Bolivia. His eyes were red rimmed by sighting the sky through the giant telescope at a twelve hour stretch, it was sunrise. He was drinking his third glass of Bolivian beer with two leaves of fresh cocaine. He could breathe as well as the natives with a concoction of leaves or chewed raw. It was better than the rancid alcoholic beer. The observatory appeared tilted on the enormous height of the peak, like a huge insect resting after a flight in the frigid night, eye opening as cupped as Venus Fly Trap was closed, and the telescope retracted for once again a probable elusive observation. Maybe he should have another beer and a handful of coca to celebrate his quest, or mission for an unnamed asteroid with erratic orbit, a concern of astronomers of the world.

The mass of the mountain was rough hewn, that of a stone carved God which might resent the steel gantry of the scope mechanism. Natives did not care, the few jobs of the observatory welcome, beside they had coca. Chris had no Gods. He was constantly reminded of his present consort, Isabella Cordova, a former chanteuse of Brazil's cabarets and cafe chantant where she sang Portuguese love songs, she almost joined a convent after a religious crisis about which he did not question. She was thirty-five, a year younger than Chris, a hefty figure of a woman but stil shapely. Her abundant hair, the color of mahogany was bound by a variety of combs. Her neck was adorned by a silver crucifix. Her eyes large and troubled, were in color secretly crying. She was his housekeeper, helping hand, cook and any hour servant. Despite, the late hour, she was sitting at his feet waiting for his next command. Chris was not unkind to think her utterly jaded. He patted Isabella on her head and demanded a cigar which she already had on hand. He lit it and leaned back. Coca and the beer kicked in, and he felt more sanguine after a disappointing observation all night long.

Chris remained in the control room of the scope in his nightly nocturne with the elusive asteroid, hoping for a sighting from the highest peak of the Andes, the glacier Chacaltya, absent minded, distracted to the point of not caring for anything else in his life. Only gradually he became aware that he and the scope had been abandoned by the staff and help by warnings from administrators and police of the advance of the rebels in the plains and valleys below the glacier. Perhaps, the scope might be an eventual target, heaven knows why. He saw from his vantage point departures of native refugees and the emptied villages. So, he was alone with his parrot, Luis. Pleasurable to him, he, the asteroid, and Luis claimed it as private possession, without gabbling talk.

The air, even in summer, sparkled with snow crystals high above most living things. He perched at seventeen thousand feet, half the size of Everest. High! Empyrean heights, Godlike, his breath rarified, his thoughts too, his imagination extraterrestrial, his dark polarized glasses all astral against the blue glaze of the glacier sight. What happened below him on a plain was ineffective to ever his purpose on the scope. The asteroid was his vacation on a peak that almost surmounted stars.

Alone, time to Chris was a heavy liquid in which he was immersed. It flowed so slowly, day and night, it hung about him like a long woolen cassock. He moved liquidly from room to console, yet whatever he timed was subject to a dozen clocks of all sizes on the walls, atomic, digital, otherwise, his life's rhythm was the ticking of a grandfather clock. But his mind was alert, so he thought he read all the signals correctly and recorded his observation with accuracy. This tempo did not impede his memory, it framed and froze samples about Montana and his family.

As a kid, his head was in the stars. From the ranch porch that was round, a rotunda, he had a three hundred and sixty degree view. The sky was often free of cumuli and the rolling hills were like a proscenium to a linen-like scrim, all step stones to a festival of stars. Only dawn with its percolating light diminished the spectacle like a Deus Ex Machina to close a performance.

Those Incan eyes that peered at him through the carved effigies! Those eyeballs tilted higher to follow the flight of a condor, their leathery cheeks like soles of battered feet, a downward look not in any abeyance, but to avoid the next cliff, and the lining of the eyes, a circle of cocaine energy. This was carved stone that fitted the arduous life of the Andes. The degraded dialects still toothlessly mumbled the grandeur of the Incan Empire.

So, after a three year tour of the astronomical sites of the world, observations lastly at the observatory in Bolivia, he had been commissioned by the United States Government and the Advance Institute of Astrophysics at Princeton, to observe, report and plot the activity and orbits of asteroids. He had been appointed because for twenty of his thirty five years he had been a leading buff of asteroids, publishing papers describing hundreds of these vagrants in space. Many raced space leaving no sign of predictive destination as they probably expunged themselves in outer space. Whenever he tagged on to one of these hurtling boulders, he predestined its fiery destiny, but there was one asteroid that eluded

3

his constant detection, its idiosyncrasy, for the last three years it occupied his devoted attention. Its vagaries perplexed him, often veering dangerously close to earth then disappearing in luminous areas of deeper distances. Streaking not with the velocity of other asteroids, it sometimes appeared to float. His only dubious guess was that it was a freak, a sport of the universe, and not an asteroid. A comet was ruled out, there was no tail, no brilliance at all, only a dusk grayness, snug-like, in his spectrum.

When he tried to explain in non-scientific terms his experience with the mysterious object, he was told he was an occultist, too many years mountain climbing and breathing the air of high altitudes had boggled his mind. He dared them to observe the object, and they did, were puzzled and happily left the study to him. A queer object in space in the pure view of a quirky astronomer, they openly deserved each other. Deployed for the last three years by the Institute in England, Australia, South Africa, China, and New Zealand, he spent his days and nights in the solitary cockpit of a giant telescope marking the course of the asteroid-like object, through the heavens, it coursed with sudden departures and appearances regardless of where he observed it from. He sighted it last week at dusk, then it appeared to evaporate. He was now thinking it had exploded, or gravitated to dust and ashes. After three years of abstruse contact, he was kind of forlorn, as if he had mistepped a companion on a voyage.

His eyes were teary, his legs cramped against the platform, his chest ached against the eyepiece of the lens. He kept wiping the eyepiece because he could not believe the gyration of the object tonight, it was like a firework out of control, at times it veered close to the earth then zoomed away scooting through the Milky Way and galaxies, metric metal and stone or a lethal plasma, a methane explosion, a miasma of suffocating and eliminating of billions on earth, and possibly extinction of all species? Including man! Of course, his colleagues thought he was a bit mad as was expected of a gifted sky watcher, when Chris once said that he thought the object was a source of language. He was thinking of it as a living thing. His contacts were sometimes unreal, palpable in some esoteric sense. This he never dared to publish, it wasn't extraterrestrial but a mano a mano. How silly. He held his head in shame and ate some more coca. Ah! A surcease for him and many others, it relieved of weariness and superstition as it had relieved the Incans of zany beliefs in Gods of the mountains. He had a compulsion to forego his specialty of asteroid and teach Astronomy 101, but he felt an organic relationship to this elf-like object.

The coca gave him acuity, he thought. He had first begun sighting the asteroid in New Zealand where he had fainted at the scope, or passed out, for two days, hardly conscious, speaking gibberish. He was brain scanned to a fault, images spoke volumes, all negative of any ischemic shadow. He recovered one morning absolutely worried about his sanity. Today, except for the consolation and assurance of coca, he was afraid that was in danger of losing his mind. All this because of a speck in the sky? Isabella tells him that the asteroid is just a mite in his eyes and nothing else.

The truth is Coca, Viva Coca! But he had to answer to his sponsors, the Institute. After all, he was not the only one observing. Numerous scientists and amateurs had sounded alarm at the nearness of this sky object and newspapers were agog with accounts of a coming Apocalypse.

Chris had been quoted by the Associated Press as saying that the shooting down of an asteroid was like shattering a flock of geese, that white down quill will be spattered with blood. Blood! No! In Space?

Chris must be mad thought Dr. Mary Gibbs of St. Elizabeth's Psychiatric Hospital in Washington, D. C., when she had been apprised of his offbeat statements. But she was inquisitive about his episode of gibberish talk, were there any discernible words, a hint, perhaps of the true nature of the asteroid-like object. She asked for a delay in the shouting match. All the world's missiles were in readiness and poised for the bareness of the entity. Science fiction buffs picketed missile sites asking for a reprieve.

His computer screen, logged onto global news, saw more items in the Prensa, Times and syndicates, about the rebel wars surrounding him and the robber barons domination of cocaine production. The picketers demanded that the missiles target them and Don Alfonso Oliviero, the Mexico rebel chief to stem the cocaine epidemic.

Graphs, photographs, charts and computer printouts of the travel log of the asteroid crammed every inch. Chris reduced his cocaine hash that made him say freakish statements to the press. He mixed a rough brew of Peruvian and Bolivian beer that roiled his empty stomach. Isabella was in extreme concern for he had not eaten in three days, as if in mourning for the coming death of his asteroid. He reluctantly ate some rice and chicken. He was sleepless and smoking cheroots of black tobacco that stunk the cockpit.

No slovenly addiction to whatever was at hand. The asteroid had given him an itch for a land of mythology, a reworking of a view of things, rerum natura. So far no bang in the sky! He rested, the drug salvaged his nerves for the time being.

There was a hubbub at the door of the console room, Isabella arguing. A camion backfired outdoors, a rare disturbance of his thoughts. A message awaited him at the door in the person of two raw soldiers of the rebel army. He was ordered to see the commander who had entered the town below to extract an annual tribute of cocaine from the farmers--none other than Don Alfonso Oliviero in person.

Chris walked a short distance to a large army truck in which stood the don, partial ruler of Peru and Bolivia. Chris was surprised at his appearance. He was dressed in a long Incan robe, that of an ascetic, his head was shaven, his face gaunt, tall standing munching coca leaf. His eyes were not glazed and unusually blue. He spoke American English with ease.

Don Alfonso Oliviero

The commander leaned on a staff of a castoff molded revolutionary flag of past revolution. Behind him was a swatch of new banners of his revolution. The scene was impressive to Chris, a graphic story, but the Commander was actually leaning on the flagstaff for support, as he had been recently wounded. His smile was kindly and inviting, encouraging, in bare van, in which he was receiving Chris. Oliviero ordered two of his men to block the entrance .

Don Alfonso strode forward to shake hands and stood beside him. The commander reeked of the jungle. His voice was high and womanish.

"Mr. Christopherson, the astroscientist?"

"I am, sir."

"You know who I am?"

"Don Alfonso Oliviero."

"I first learned of you at the University of Mexico where I studied medicine. I am a professor, like yourself, not of astronomy, pediatrics. I practiced for ten years in the slums of Mexico City for free, then, I became a rebel, not a Maoist, but a genuine revolutionary, Mr. Christopherson. When your eyes were in the stars mine were on the star grit of this earth. Now, once a secure professor you have become a pariah like myself. You belong in the jungle with me, and

7

why? We passionately believe in the compatibility of our individual soul to an animalistic loving nature. You followed the asteroid, I understand, as it was willful, as I had it in mind, it defied physical laws, it turned at right angle like a dragon fly." He paused realizing his effect.

"Your mouth is open, in amazement that I know you so well. I read your report in the New York Times."

"Did you observe it by chance?" Chris shook his head as if trying to focus.

"Whatever it is, I agree with you that the object is harmless."

"Thank you, you do realize we are practically alone in that opinion." Chris laughed nervously.

"Lives here have existed at these high altitudes for centuries in a steady diet with leaf that invigorates the blood, stimulates energy for the tedium vitae of work. I have captured three quarters of the coca crop of South America. I have waged war against traffickers, governments, robbers, and international bankers to stop the deadly traffic of cocaine and derivatives. The indiscriminate use has killed millions of people. In my domain I allocate so much coca leaf per person to all, to help with old age, weariness of body and spirit and painful suffering. It is a prescribed dosage. This is what I intend for mankind if they allow me to live a bit longer, the Buddha has failed! I might succeed concerning suffering but I cannot answer the last question at Unction time," he adjusted for balance on his staff wincing.

"You are a saint!"

"Me? I am the illegitimate child of a sixteen year old girl. I have twenty pediatricians on my staff."

" Bless you that you are not willing to stain space with blood!"

"Perhaps, a service. I must leave now. I have removed the guards from the observatory. No one will impede your work. You are free to use it. We shall meet again I am sure, that is, if we survive a reputed catastrophe," he glanced upwards, then continued eyeing Chris with medical scrutiny,

"Aword before I take my leave. I have noted that you over use the coca. We have spies, my dear friend, stay within my prescribed dosage and you will live a long life. Farewell, Amigo. You are safe--for now. I have contained the area with my troops, but we are in retreat and in great need of rest."

Oliviero turned as if to break off, then spun around to address Chris in a softer tone, "One more word! You have met me, I am no villain. Who are we? Are we true rebels, not drug traffickers, nor corrupt Federales, world war remnants of grand traditions of the revolution of Madero, Bolivar and Zapata. We are considered jackals of the jungle. We are hunted by the Federals and drug traffickers. We have retreated here on the slope of the glacier for recouping but we shall be attacked soon. My men have restocked your supplies. We prefer death to defeat. Goodbye!"

Chris returned to the observatory dazed by the encounter, drained by the coursing of adrenalin through his system. He collapsed onto his futon and slept.

Chris returned to the control room and computer keyboard. He opened the cover revealing a pinpoint sky. How long had he slept? The sky was darkening and welcoming him back. It was so like the upper pasture at the ranch, he knew where every blade of grass was and where the weeds. So he searched for the fugitive once again. Suddenly, he saw ominous streaks across the sky and in space. Three missiles fired at a hazy target exploding with no contact. Chris clapped his hands with satisfaction. They must have used his calculations on the coordinates of the last asteroid sighting, but it was elsewhere. Where? The missile technicians could not qualify how they had miscalculated from the available information.

Chris relaxed, lit a cheroot, and mused on his conversation with Don Alfonso. Why seek him out?

He focused the scope on the sky quadrant. There it was, peeping from behind the moon! He stood up as if to wave it back, he heard himself shout 'Get Back!' Missile finders were roving the universe. It returned to the back of the moon as if it had heard his cry.

On the top he was in touch with the bottoms of the world. Three months went by in nightly sighting of the sky looking for the roving or now stationary asteroid behind the moon. The sound of warfare rebounded off the mountain surfaces. He had no money. He had been dismissed by all peremptory, but whatever he needed was provided by rebel guards deputized by Oliviero, a corporal and six soldiers. Although he read his Kepler, it was singular distraction between shy asteroid and the rumble of civil war. As the months went by rumors of the rebels defeat in multiple encounters reached him. He began to realize what he was amid was not a civil war but an international war. The excuse was that the rebels were actually traffickers in coca and other drugs and depredators of civilized cities and towns without a vow for collective action to introduce a risky colonial justice to a revived concept of charity. But charity is one man's balm and another man's bane. The rebels were being routed not by militia but virtual mercenaries of several nations. Bombed from the air, decimated by small missile fire, and incendiaries, they were aflame. They however, did not destroy the coca crops reserved for their own ends, charity in the jungle is the surreal air of the peak?

Chris could not see from his vantage point that the rebels were in retreat but his guards were withdrawn. Isabella told him that Oliviero had been assassinated by one of his own bodyguard of paid killers. At the end of the month of nervy hostilities, ragged groups of rebels entered the town and vicinity of the observatory and wherever possible bivouacked.

The Little Colonel

The head of the straggling soldiers was a twenty-six year old woman with the stripes of a colonel, although beleaguered by defeat. She was curious about the telescope and sought the occupant of whom Oliviero had spoken.

Chris met her halfway and escorted her to his office quarters. He was surprised at how petite she was. No rebel uniform would possibly fit so she dressed as she liked, shorts, heavy woolen blouse with epaulets, an automatic pistol at her side, prominent breast for a small female, a pretty face with a pinched look of care and command. She displayed an overall stance of defiance, but she relaxed and sat beside him on the futon, her legs shapely in worn boots. She stretched, and yelled the rebel yell, which shook Chris. Chris almost lunged towards her so eager was he for human company. She held up her hands as to ward off an assault, a pistol pointed at his chest. She immediately understood the action and lowered the pistol and laughed broadly. It appeared she too was eager and pleased to speak to an American in virtual exile like herself, only cooped in a cockpit of a telescope., By this exchange, they relaxed, she with weariness, he with the tedium of sky watching day and night.

Frank Palescandolo

She took another deep breath. Chris expected another rebel yell, but she smiled cracked lips, and spoke clearly not in Spanish or Portuguese but in a New England twang.

"I am an Americana renegade."

"I can tell, Massachusetts? New Hampshire?" Chris raised his eyebrows and looked to the side.

She threw up her arms. "What am I doing here?"

"You said you are a renegade."

"I am as American as apple pie, Christopherson. Amherst, joined the Youth Corps after graduation. I was assigned to Bogota. I worked for three years in the slums of the poorest country side. I was supposed to help the Incans, teach them the English language and our customs. I really tried," she sighed as deeply as anybody could. "I found nothing but vile politicians, corruption, rackets, prostitution and all drug trafficking aided by the Federales. What was my choice. You are in the midst of things happening. I had to make a bare choice, return defeated or remain to better conditions. My conscience spoke loudly to remain and join the forces rebelling against the disastrous situation. My family, the State Department recalled me. They believed I had gone native. But by then I had already resigned the Youth Corps and gotten my first commission under the command of Don Alfonso Oliviero, the saint!" she stood up abruptly and saluted him.

"I am Abigail Simpson at your service. What can I do for you while I am here?" She did not pause for his reply, " I cannot rest long because my remaining troops and I are in line for a show down with Drug Enforcement Army at the river in two days. Perhaps this will be then last stand for the remnants of Oliviero's army. Perhaps I will be captured. Perhaps repatriated as a kooky Yankee, back in the bosom of my family, while down the street drug peddlers are making their buck and bankers, their millions." Abigail closed her eyes deep in reflections of another reality,

12

"Oliviero once said, 'A rebel always a rebel, you were born crying out, loud protesting, vulgarity of shit and blood. So, I shall be off! I know some think you a rebel, but I don't see you as that." She spoke so rapidly that Chris could all but follow her train of thought.

"By the way, where is your wandering asteroid now?"

"Behind the moon!"

"That's a safe place these days. Is it waiting to impact the earth as your colleagues claim? Will you relent and save this Amherst girl from extinction?"

"The asteroid is not my invention." Chris answered defensively.

"Those who pray," she raised her eyes to the ceiling, "may I have your autograph?"

Chris too confused to do else wise, he jotted his initials on a scrap computer printout and handed it to her. Abigail folded it and stuffed in a breast pocket. She gave him a ragged epaulet.

Abigail placed a letter in his hands addressed to her mother and sisters in Massachusetts. "Please mail my letter. You may read it."

Abigail sat down next him. He placed the epaulet in his lap and read the letter openly.

'My heart was hardened but my revolutionary spirit is encouraged. I made a good choice. I was Christianized a true rebel. Oliviero says I am a fatalist. I deny it to him, but I believe we shall fail. I have been company with evil in its worst aspects, not metaphysical, but as a deep defect in human nature that is difficult to make do with goodness. My experience with death, when I shot dead a soldier at my feet was an attack of a fever which lasted two days. What was it, this fever? It was shame that reddened my body with stigmata. I saw that terror of nightmares had overcome reality. I am better now. I am the molded soldier trained to kill. However, I have not changed. I am still that tomboy who jumped fences. Keep my books intact. Give my Phi Beta key to little Jane and Sarah my copy of Edna Millay. I hope to write further, you are in my heart, all of you. Don't forget to give Nellie her shots and groom her, nails need care. Until the next letter-- Love."

This 'letter' of Abigail's was actually jottings on the spot of action, probably written at some intervals in the fighting and consisted of loosely held sheaves of odd paper. He read on through extensive passages with double interest?

'From the first day in camp I was inspired by Commander Oliviero's loyalty to the decent causes of bygone revolutions in the Andes, his gentleness and yet vigor in combat. Before any encounter he pleaded with the enemy for peace, brotherhood, made every effort to spare bloodshed on either side. At first, I became one of a number of international recruits like Janissaries, shared the rigor of training in the jungle and the hot plains. I climbed the steepest mountain with my male comrades. Shoulder to shoulder, in a skirmish I was a standout in that I rescued several buddies in an ambush. I was rewarded with my first command. I fell in love, he was killed. I fell in love, he was decapitated. I fell in love, he was killed by a land bomb.'

Chris paused to recover his breath, realizing he was hyperventilating.

Abigail stood up and look down upon him beseechingly, " I am going to battle. We are outnumbered, outgunned. I am not sure I will survive. This diary of sorts is an accounting of what really happened. I do not wish it to fall into the hands of the enemy. I want my family to have it and I cannot get it to them. I have not heard from them in five years in this jungle. So, I must explain who I am for they love me, my sisters and my mother. There is a gulf of misunderstanding that must be erased before I die. I had to do what I did. I must love my life as it is, Amor Fati. I must love my life to live it. I entrust this to you. Please!" She left with a click of heels!

Oliviero believed that good men recognized each other almost instantly. It seemed they lived in a compassionate realm although the rebel force was involved in a bare boned warfare from Bogota to cells all over South America, and elsewhere. All brothers in a spirit of change, by revolution, of justice, peasant and underclass of developing countries rebelling in wars against plutocratic occupation and remnants of colonialism, and exploitation of native populations.

Chris has no agenda in mind, he was an asteroid devotee for twenty years and paid little mind to mundane affairs. He was modern normally, a disinterested scientist except in his own specialty. Now, however, he was caught between the two, in his telescope, between his timid asteroid and the fury below him in the jungles, valleys and plains of South America.

When he turned his telescope and adjusted his lens to nearness he could sight on the fire fights in dense jungles, skirmishes in the plains and the explosions in nearby cities. He focused on vast fields of cultivated coca in fertile areas occupied by the guerillas controlling the disposition of the crops for the benefit of the populace, out of the hands of worldwide traffickers, and lobbyists. He had not sought to join sides in the conflict but let's face it, 'Christopherson, you were a guerilla scientist from this day even in the isolation of his telescope cockpit and the neutral skies above.'

Isabella was still at his beck and call. The edifice of the telescope included two bedrooms, a small living space and a galley for cooking. Isabella occupied one room and he the other, a narrow corridor connected them. That evening, Chris invited Isabella to look in the lens, but she balked. The heavens were his business, and hers, his survival. On these long nights, he asked her to sing a Portuguese song, but she remained close lipped and refused. Love was a very faded rose in her heart which was a song in itself, thought Chris.

From his cubicle the world was in the control of drug lords and illicit bankers who were laundering vast sums of money, nation's treasuries in the greed of rot, greed that appeared to be universal. Wars flared on every certainty and no ideology. Africa was a further pit of genocide, religions were fractious, assassinating each other with the blessing of a precept or other. The seas had become vicious with oil spills and contaminants from open sewers. The rarest thing to find was a true trout stream in which trout could breathe oxygen. He was witness via the glowing computer screen focused on today's global news.

Chris wondered that perhaps during these three years of vigilance and observation, that the asteroid did not want to witness this spiritual and natural disaster. It was blind behind the moon. Was he sure it was so? That pitiful worm, that grown up germ, that two legged monster that ravished, that predator that killed its own. Titan still ruled the earth devouring his own children, driving all innocent animals to extinction. Man!

No mythologies of beauty and transience, no belief that was not based on advantage and co-opting. What ruled was money and faddism.—a faddism of entertainment. Rulers were actors, actresses or rock stars. Idols were muscular men and shapely women. Sex was a pastime, motherhood an old maid's fancy, and that's all. Pornography was only second to the drug trade as a source of immense wealth and power. Pusillanimous poets and sanctimonious pundits, and people left with the consolations of the meaningless, conspicuous and non-historical life of TV. Yes, of course, the heroes of nightly viewing. With the sense of honorable history gone, that gave credit to man in great civilizations, a general atavism in the arts prevailed. There was little respect for the word, and poetry and metaphysics. All drama poor in human dialogue was petty partisan monologues of empty minds. Music had become electronic noise, not white noise, disruptive to every cell of the human body.

And the whales, what did they have to grin about in the once mythic depths of the seas. Dolphins leapt in vapid air. To Chris, it appeared to him through reflection that the planet itself had turned color from green to an eerie yellow.

Chris upped his dosage of the remaining coca and smoked terminal cheroots. He distilled quantities of coca to still Isabella's pain as she was suffering from breast cancer. Still she did her chores. She died one night of kidney failure. From her papers he deduced that she had abandoned two children to further her career as a danseuse.

He was alone in his cubicle, four years older, graying fast, gaunt as aging leather, his nose flaked by the use of coca. If not for the coca he would have hurled himself from the peak into the abyss below. He was never the suicidal type but really from his vantage point he saw no hope for his planet, he had less concern for man which he now despised utterly. For company, he had Luis, his bulk gray parrot, who was affectionate and craved petting and attention. The parrot also loved puzzles and distractions, intelligent enough to unravel twine, block mechanisms of rattles and toys, and always with a quizzical turn of the head, he asked for Chris' soft caress, which he received in kind from the perched bird. When he let him out of the cage some afternoons he would imitate Chris and attempt to peer through the scope. Did it make sense to an affectionate parrot as to what he might have seen?

In a jar, in a cupboard, he found a gummy lump of opium and a pipe. Why not, he had not slept well for a week. He filled the pipe, lit it and lay down to sleep which happened soon. He dreamed not of hours dancing in Paradise, but of thousands of shimmering sheep grazing on the family ranch on a sunny afternoon.

His nights were almost Artic.

The Cloud

It was the year 2010 when it happened. It was a frigid night in February. Luis' cage was hooded from the chill. He had a small heater at his stand. The telescope creaked open in subzero temperatures and for the millionth time he focused the scope on the probable whereabouts of his asteroid.

Chris first sighted the moon that shone with glacial fullness in the sky. It was the last redoubt of the asteroid. He saw it! Yes! In his excitement he upset the cage of the alarmed parrot. He saw it! It was peeking from behind the moon, now moving in his direction, in a dazed projection towards earth. Was the asteroid serious in its intention to destroy the planet or was it once again a tease? Fooling? But with increasing velocity it was approaching him on a direct line. He lost sight, as if a syncopee had stopped his heart. If so, he was dying an ecstatic death.

The velocity of the asteroid was incalculable, stalling, unimaginatively, it coursed through the etherized space towards earth. How can he possibly imagine the size, the immensity of the impact? Nothing left but fire and ashes, and grit of the once gem-like planet of the Universe!

Chris laughed shrilly to himself. "Come on," he screamed. "Incinerate me interstellar fire, rid me of whatever remains as man!"

Despite his bravado existential fears gripped his heart. The scientist nonetheless seized the moment. After all these years, what was the asteroid like before it hits the earth. Many months he thought the asteroid was unreal. But real, it was coming on faster and faster. It passed the missile barrier, the speed was unmatchable, the size of a moons' satellite now, in the closing atmosphere there was no trail, no sign of friction within earth's envelope. Frictionless? No conceivable matter at all? How was that possible, yet an object in its form hurtled on heading for earth. As it came near it appeared to pulse like an organism, not plasma. A giant heartbeat? No time for alarm, the earth was doomed. Doomed!

He hugged Luis' cage. It was here now. He thought he felt a jolt, the crash! The end! The object braked above his head with no contact with earth, blocking out most starlight into cerulean twilight.

"A Cloud!" exclaimed Chris holding his heart, 'It was an immense cloud?"

No blast, no heat, no fission, no sound at all except for a silence like breathing. The Cloud pulsated rhythmically. Still the scientist, Chris noted with care the phenomenon that hovered above earth.

All electrical systems were shut down and energy grids were short circuited. All communication muted throughout the world. Except for Chris. His throat was crammed with uncontrollable gibberish reminiscent of that attack of years ago. The force of the pressure threatened to burst through the crown of his cranium. Slowly, the gibberish became clear translation. A childish voice resounded.

"Mr. Christopherson, my friend, do not fear us. We confide in you. You have been chosen to be our spokesman to the people of the Earth. We are a race, the millions of unborn children, aborted, abandoned and slain. Below us our putative fathers, mothers, cousins, nephews, uncles, aunts, nannies, so we come not for purposes of revenge and vindication but out of our need for reaffirmation by love to recommend remedies for man's unnatural cruelties to himself, to animals, and life itself. The earth is darkness at noon. All will be panicked beyond their senses, but they must be attentive to you, our chosen spokesman."

There was a long pause, then, the voice continued. "This is no sermon from the mount, we do not speak repent. We are too proud of our own innocence to reprove you beyond reason. We were deprived of love, of life. It is our purity, our innocence which compels us to save man from further villain. We are not space fiction. We are driftless children in a cold complex. We come to say that your souls and your lives are in peril." Chris squinted and rubbed his ears to ease the pressure in his head. He welcomed the pause to adjust his breathing.

The voice, renewed in strength, continued. "We speak of love, but we can be pitiless if man continues the abominations of slaughter, warfare and degradation. There is the Law over which we have no control. So listen well to our counsel and conditions for survival. We shall return to speak of these in twelve hours. In the meantime, search for your consciences, search deeply, past and present. We require rigorous self examination for contrition, acquiescence to mysterious, not so mysterious power. All things living and dead," the pulsing appeared to distance itself.

The world was devoid of artificial light, except for Chris, who seemed to be privileged. All were steeped in an eerie twilight that allowed a daub of starlight alone to illumine a vague horizon.

The earth seemed immobile, as if it were deep in pitch of untamable remorse, of frozen fright and terror.

Chris could see from where he was no intelligible response, just a constant wailing from billions of throats. The lighting of millions of votive candles, instant pilgrimages, churches overflowing with prayers and petitions for an Earthly purgatory. Yet, the Cloud had not spoken of accepted purgatory or hinted at the purging of wrong doing and wrong thinking. The children seemed to be innocent of theology. The guide was love that craved in return their due. If he listened carefully, he heard occasionally, the prattle of children from on high.

How could one account for the eloquence of the message? Many geniuses were unborn, Chris speculated.

Luis squawked for attention, but Chris was busy taking account of his own life and did not attend to him as usual. Upon introspection, what did he see? A man one minded in the pursuit of an asteroid minding nothing else, family or children. He never harmed anyone intentionally. He was not a churchgoer although he did not sense the Cloud insistent on that point. He was a good son. He was in the habit of praying to a sunrise.

The childish voice began again. "Attention Earth! The council of the Cloud has consulted and concluded that, in fairness, before any hasty condemnation for crimes you have committed, there shall be a trial, visible to all. We need time to establish a formal intelligible indictment. The trial will be a military tribunal. The courtroom will be at the United Nations in New York City. The tribunal shall consist of nine judges who will be dogs. Dogs will handle the prosecution and cats will be the animal curiae. Defense counsel will be an elder Clyde Bourne horse. Animals will participate as immediate audience. The members of the American Kennel Club will be Sergeant at Court and general factotums."

And then it was over. Silence! Chris had been an agnostic but he did not believe that mattered so much to the children, ignorant of the tinkering of belief. Did the children require the redemption of man's divinity? He slumped over his console in a state of complete mental exhaustion and slept in unconscious stupor.

The Trial of Man

humongous sky screen was lit, its luminescence a floating mirage, visible all over the globe. In twilight, Chris could not hope to describe the condition of the world's population. He would have to collate the news channels of that day for an idea of the turmoil. The people appeared to squirm like worms for every safety niche on earth, in caves, in churches, in monasteries, in universities, in subway systems. The Apocalyptic buffs hailed the Cloud's coming at street corners.

"You ask who will speak for the Court? The answer is the judges shall be empowered to speak the English language and will be translated into one hundred and eight nine languages representing the accused sovereignties and citizens. There will be no appeal from a verdict ultimately handed down by the nine member tribunal. I shall introduce them."

Then on that screen was displayed the vast interior of the United Nations Assembly. Seen was the tribunal and in it were seated the Chief Judge and President, Best in Show for three years at the Westminster Dog Show at Madison Square Garden, Governor Maritime, a Newfoundland. Next to him a Vice President, Best of Breed at the Morris and Essex Show, Aspen, a Saint Bernard. Best of Show at Boston, Maximillian, a Great Dane. Best of Breed at San Franciso, Nose Dive, a Boston Terrier. Best of Show at

Munich, Count Russ, a Boxer. Best of Breed at Moscow, Ivana, Russian Wolfhound. Best of Show at Torino, Garibaldi, an Italian Greyhound. These dogs all champions time and time again. The art, the top of the canine breed! Secondly, but not least, the prosecuting team is led by Fritz Von Lepzig, German Shepherd, Best of Breed at Beijing this year. Animus curiae will be led by Wilhelmina Kutz, Queen Cat of the Year. The defense team leader is renowned Clyde Bourne, Bruce of Sussex. We shall excuse a Grand Jury for the prosecution believes it has sufficient proof of its indictment."

And so the trial began. Chris glued to the screen. There was no jury. The proceedings were likened to a Court Martial where members of the Tribunal had the final say.

This was a Blue Ribbon Court with no pun intended. Seated in the tribunal were canine champions of the highest integrity, devotion, loyal and obedient, paragons of special beauty.

Fritz Von Lepzig, the German Shepherd drew himself to his full height and spoke.

"To prepare an adequate indictment one would have to recreate the crimes you may have committed only during the last years. That of course is impossible so I beg your indulgence to say that I shall provide simulacra of those occurrence through new clips, video recordings, war department photography and computer data which we have subpoenaed. Many of you were not present or near these atrocities and deception of national and personal interest and welfare, but you often accepted the reputed facts without challenge and went smugly back to your selfish slumbers. Do not turn your eyes away if you find the raw facts and scene unbearable to watch. This is your trial and you are entitled to view every bit of evidence presented against you. Some of the secret conclusions have never seen the light of day. We have combed the sainted libraries of Presidents, dictators, to extract—what ," he paused to inhale deeply, "Yes, the truth."

With sideways glance and pointing of his ears in the direction of the defense counsel, he continued, "I anticipate that the defense counsel will object that these documents are highly prejudicial to the defendant's case. Mr. Clyde Bourne is a gentle horse of most mild disposition, and a little too fond of man, and he will remonstrate despite his distaste to defend you. Using this remote control, I will have access to this full data base and will display all on the global screen. There will be no commentary or caption because I cannot find words to describe the horror that you will preview. So we shall begin."

The defense counsel in a weak bray said, "But aren't there just wars?"

The prosecutor rose to object. "Of course, Mr.Counsel that is an oxymoron."

Meekly, the defense counsel responded, "I am only repeating what has been said from the highest place of judicial science."

"You have been to the wrong school," growled the prosecutor impatiently.

"They have principles."

"Principles? No Principles," said the prosecutor with a curling lip.

The stallion looked about him for help, to his staff. He had trouble making eye contact in the first place. He had only accepted the post out of duty to the animal fraternity. He personally abhorred the actions of human beings, but he was fond of his owner and trainer who treated him well. So, within his own paddock he was smug, that is, as long as there were mares in the next stall. It was crude, but he was a renowned sire and the thought of any of his offspring being killed was horrendous, it made him rear in fury. He regained his composure as the prosecutor began again.

Von Lepzig was indomitable. "What convinces a man or woman to kill, what justification, what reason, what credo? Why is there this lack of love in their breasts? One would think that as with all

24

animals there would be a visceral repulsion at killing your own kind. You demonize each other so you can pretend you are not killing your fellowman, you demonize to excoriate your guilt as we crush an unwitting insect."

Tenacity was a sterling quality of the German Shepherd breed and it was ever evident as he continued, "People of the world, look at each other with an element of fear. The population of the earth, mostly illiterate has been lead into criminality by the sociable clerks, the elected and the powerful. Citizens, innocent, have been lied to and traduced by immoral leaders-- plebes, untouchables, poor, unemancipated, good people. I say redeem the villains, alive or dead, that would be fair and justice will be served. The Cloud demands the soul be recaptured and express itself in virtue." A pail of water was beside his desk, and he lapped at it thirstily to refresh himself, regaining his composure he rose on unsteady legs.

"What kind has allowed the young to die, remanded to the Cloud, with never a touch. Man has abrogated the instincts of all animals, not to kill his own species. Instead, you memorialize atrocity with monuments and geriatric honors. What negated this instinct.? Man has been misled. He has been told he has the right to express individual right without morality. Survival of the fittest! That a race is inferior! Man has been damaged by nations, genders confused, egoism rules and money, their invisible God."

Then as a climax, he clicked the remote and there was a panning of video files of thousands of abortion clinics throughout the world with waiting lines of young women and men.

The Vice President of the Tribunal, Aspen the Saint Bernard, stood on a point of order and addressed the Court.

"Please note for the record that we have cut off the sound of the world's wailing, crying and execration, the plaints for forgiveness which the prosecution feels may influence the tribunal and the Cloud's judgment."

The screen illuminated once more. The sight was of the vermin, mud and maimed flesh of thirty thousand soldiers, scattered bones of the Somme, Verdun and its toll.

The defense counsel Bruce of Sussex fainted and fell to the ground with a thud. He was too good hearted and not suited for this job. He was summarily replaced with an Arabian Stallion, Abdullah. A forklift was provided to remove the Clyde Bourne off to a huge couch in the outer hall.

The evidence resumed.

Flashes in rapid fire burst upon the screen: Piave, the Marne, Ardennes, the Hindenburg Clash, the Russian Revolution, the American Civil War, the Belgian Congo, Auschwitz, Buchenvald, the bombing of Hamburg, the Blitz of London, Nagasaki, Hiroshima, carpet bombing of Vietnam—napalm viscous over all. Somalia, Iraq, Afghanistan, the World Trade Towers. Indiscriminate carnage, men and women and millions of animals. It was like a majoring dark piano rolling before the world's eyes.

Screaming decibels of anguished cries, and explosions, so many explosions, the hobby of the twentieth century shattered the ear. And for hours, the populace watched with no escape into side exits the graphic intensity of the horror of recent generations.

The only reply was dry vomit.

A hippodrome was needed to curb the panic of the equines in the flares of bombing and incineration. A fledging or two strayed among the birds looking for parents and a protected nest. The emotions of the animals were displayed in the frothing at the lips, shivering as if in shock and a mournful crooning from the others.

Abdullah wiped his eyes. Aides though he was also taking ill. Two grooms supported him, he managed to say, "Sirs, that I am speechless, I know no law that I can cite as prejudice for mercy, but I do plead mercy as it is my duty.

Governor Maritime recessed the court until six in the evening.

At the appointed time, the screen was illuminated once more. The courtroom was visible to all. Everyone was seated and an uneasy calm settled. The judges marched in and sat back satisfied with their verdict.

Garibaldi, the Italian Greyhound, acting as secretary of the Tribunal handed the verdict to the Clerk of the Court, Brutus, the piebald ivory tusked elephant, who waited anxiously.

Brutus trumpeted the verdict! Guilty! The rafters shook as if with sonic boom.

Lions and Tigers in the bottom row caterwauled and mewed sorrowfully, wiping their face with open paws. One water buffalo on a side seat trampled a table in outrage. Everywhere, a doglike gravity in the proceedings. A giraffe, the recording secretary, sat ungainly cross-legged before a whiskey.

There was a massive soughing of birds; canaries, swallows, finches, larks, ducks, orioles, swans, birds of paradise, brilliant macaws, nightingales, a tremendous chorale that was dissonant, but harmonious heralding promise. Bowers of flowers appeared in the balconies of the grand hall. The braying of horses added to the chorale.

The Newfoundland used no gavel but a giant paw which banged the tribunal table and demanded order to stop the whimpering and sniffling of the creatures.

The Vice President, Aspen was woozy having sipped from the brandy cask about his neck, a Pyrenees joined him. They managed to nod soberly. Someone proposed an anthem for the event, but there was no mood at all for music.

Edicts of the Cloud

"**M**ankind! The following are the conditions of your sentence as assessed by the Cloud." It was Chris' visage on the screen and his voice exaggerated a thousand fold.

"First, all abortion must cease, there must be reverence.

In every aspect war is abolished. There are no just wars, or for any reason, warfare is condemned.

No genocide will be tolerated. It is abhorrent to human sensibility.

There will be representative government that will equally represent every citizen.

States rights will be respected to protect local interests and eliminate centralized tyranny.

Urbanization will be discouraged to support pasteurization and green interests.

Communal living will be fostered by limiting the construction of additional high speed highway systems that obliterate small communities.

Universities shall be places of learning and culture.

The school system must concentrate on career and trade training and search for talent despite academic prowess.

There shall be renewed respect of craftsmanship.

There shall be a justifiable discrepancy in wages with no plutocratic excesses.

The structure of jurisprudence must be simplified and the force of lawyers must be limited

Money must not be allowed to influence elections.

There will be no state execution whatsoever.

There will be national banks devoted to fiduciary responsibility for the finance and economy.

Pornography in any form will not be allowed.

Every citizen will be entitled to free medical attention.

Every citizen is guaranteed economic security through the sharing of dividends from the annual proceeds of nations.

And, too, each citizen will be entitled to a prescribed dosage of cocaine for the benefit of his health and relief of pain and existential anxiety."

The Cloud moved a bit, casting a longer shadow across the earth and makeshift courtroom. Once more and not again did the listening world hearing the chattering of children from above. An adult voice, Chris, intervened and the chattering dutifully ceased.

"We are not avenging or vindictive angels. We still remember the little love you gave us as you caressed your bellies an afternoon. We are here to correct your criminal ways. Mr. Chris Christopherson, who has been a companion of ours for many year's will be our ombudsman. If these edicts are not obeyed we shall incinerate you to oblivion."

"We have watched for limitless years as children watch their children. We are bound to fidelity and love. We hope to bind you to us. We shall insist on these conditions for your redemption, not so much for what is called sin, but divine justice."

"All the governments and sovereign ties will be proxies for the billions of their citizens from whom we seek compliance." The voice changed, younger with a lispish lilt.

"We yearn to love--although we were not loved. We therefore convoked in a Court of Supreme love to try you for your crimes to life itself. You have been convicted, the animal kingdom, your judges. We have not known pity, but pity the billions seduced by money and fake glory. We cannot allow you to return to your existence of profit and selfishness, relentless greed and homicidal habit."

There was a long pause, then, another youthful voice boomed, "No! These are the conditions to which you must comply. We will give you a probationary period of twenty years within which to remake your ways by complying with all edicts. We shall return to judge the results. Do not fail, for if you do you will no longer be a part of the Universe."

As the Cloud lifted, the sky turned roseate as their shadow retreated to its refuge behind the moon. The judges nodded to each other. If they could kiss each other, the animals would have.

The sky screen scanned the swarming cities of the Earth. Guilt, suicide and death cast a pall over the cities, towns and villages. Everyone awed by the decree of impending death. A wave of communication rolled like a giant tsunami. Billions of hands were uplifted in supplication to the ever present Cloud. Millions covered themselves with ashes of repentance. They were negotiable. What power could ever forgive them?

Chris bowed his head humbly. Reverent acquiescence.

Then, there was a deafening roar of approval, of endorsement of the conditions of the sentence! A titanic sigh of relief swept the courtroom and the world. This was not incineration, it was reprieve, a time allowed for reformation and rejuvenation in the vitality of life and the compassion of disenfranchised children

He realized that through the proclamation of the edicts of the Cloud, that he did not close his eyes in one wink as if he had been under a hypnotic sway. This sense of his body being transposed in that of the Cloud had totally overwhelmed his normal perceptions.

He thought he sensed a thank you from the Cloud, like a tip of a hat.

With a flash of light the worldwide sky screen blackened.

Early Reviews

His voice had been returned to him, he tested it. He took a deep breath, he was famous, a celebrity, discoverer of the asteroid and now the spokesman for the Cloud. The only person in their opinion privileged to carry their message. How to collaborate? No clique or bombast. He picked up three leaves of his cache of coca, chewed slowly and mused. Luis, annoyed at being ignored for many hours, nudged him. Chris stroked the back of Luis' head.

Chris had no children, no responsibility, yet he adored children. He thoroughly enjoyed his time conducting programs in the Planetarium for them, part of his duties while on a fellowship in graduate school. He looked forward to the elementary school children's visits, especially the eager curiosity and eye wide wonder as the dome revealed the glittering heavens. The children accepted the sight without any doubts or fear as he ushered them into the Universe. They bubbled questions. He always had candy on hand and small prizes, and pats on tousled heads. His disliked domesticity, his home was in the heavens. Was he the favorite of the children in the Cloud? Chris did not think so perhaps it was just that he was their first friend.

But, today, in the dimly lit chamber of the observatory, he was part of the masses in the Stygian panic. Maimed and disfigured children could not set him apart from the calumny of carnage and history. He was tainted by the blasphemies of the past generations just like everyone else.

Would he have the moral strength to respond to this spectacle? Chris promised himself he would try, lending whatever faculty he had, to accommodate the Cloud, to be its servant, there was no challenge, really. Hadn't he always been? He patted his cache of coca with a deep sigh. It exuded a strong spirit, who knows if the general was correct in his promotion of King Coca of the Andes?

What was there to do now, but wait? In the meantime, his only link to what was going on elsewhere on Earth was known to him through his radio and computer screen.

From what Chris could see, the Earth was a crawling concatenation of millions thronging to shrines, temples, any holy place, seeking safety. Self-flagellants lashed themselves along revered avenues, pilgrims climbed cathedral step on bare knees. No madness but a sense of ineluctable doom.

Video fragments flashed manically across his screen. Parliaments, Congresses, Presidents, Premiers, Prime Ministers, the Joint Chiefs of Staff, Third World Dictators , the NY Stock Exchange, World Bank, Supreme Courts of Law. Commentary everywhere. So many speeches to describe the indescribable.

Chris looked on soberly. Did mankind have so little confidence in its own resources to change in accordance with the Cloud's edicts, already?

The Incan Mayor

When he awakened there was work to be done. The world and the nations were growing in turmoil facing imaginable and unimaginable problems.

Chris thought of his family, his parents, brothers, and sisters, congeries of cousins. How are they reacting in Montana? He printed out the latest local news from his hometown. The state was in place. Vast pastures were green and the sheep on the higher slopes at this time of year, mountains unmoved. Small towns, were huddling in conference. Response to his earlier email indicated everyone was managing as best as could be expected at the Ranch. They were all proud of Chris' role as the spokesman, but afraid for him. His first girlfriend just had a baby boy, her first. Chris responded that he believed that the Cloud was not vindictive but wished to rain love upon the heads of humankind. He, had his parrot and coca.

The sky was clear at sundown. Chris supported himself on the console smoking a cheroot. Luis was on his shoulder, both gazed up at a Western sky, all rosy. One by one the stars emerged. He rounded them up, like a sheepdog herding the sheep into a sheep fold, where he could justify himself an astronomer, he knew he could never corral the Cloud. This was a momentary aberration.

Chris' thoughts turned to his more immediate circumstance. Through his sighting device, Chris could see down the valley where hundreds of bodies were ravished by crows and wolves.

Mother revolution was out of control! And the petite colonel? Her diary was in his breast pocket.

There was a loud knock at the door. Chris opened the door cautiously. Standing before him was the Mayor of the local village, he had met him before. He was an old man half Incan who was smoking a pipe and chewing a cud. His eyes were ringed with black splotches, he had not slept well. He hunched a blanket about him and kneeled before Chris.

"Sir, we are in your hands, have mercy."

"Father, I am man, too!"

"You are more than any man. You are favored by the Cloud. You have nothing to fear, you are innocent. You must promise to protect us."

"I shall advise you as best I can, I have your welfare at heart."

"Thank you, thank you, sir. There is one thing that troubles me deeply."

"And that is?"

"The fate of our coca! As you know coca has meant our survival for centuries. It has given us hope, strength and vigor to endure the Andes. What is proposed by the Edict of the Cloud is to provide coca for all, which will industrialize the use and practice of coca throughout the world. As you know there are vast organizations committed to the exploitation of coca, the Mexican cartels, Bolivian, Peruvian, wherever coca is grown. Millions of people have been enslaved by the abuse of the beneficial coca. The distribution will be mismananged. We believe we shall be robbed of our inheritance. Already our countryside is being wasted by the battles between Federal troops and the rebels. There has been a massacre below." the mayor's head was in his hands and he swayed trying to keep his balance, and began again,

"The rebels are our peasants. Some are fighting for the preservation of their ancestral rights for the cultivation of coca and its customs. In truth, coca is a practical religion. The armies oppose the rebels and armies are bankrolled by investors in addiction and death. The rebels are dying by the hundreds. Our village has lost one hundred of its citizens. At the foot of the mountain and the jungle edge lie the slain and unburied." His face twisted in horror.

"I have seen the carnage with my scope." Chris interrupted the Mayor.

"The stench has driven the lamas away, only magpies and vultures are there feeding on carrion."

Chris thought again of Abigail Simpson with a pang. She was probably among them. He squeezed his eyes to make the vision go away.

The Mayor composed himself and continued, "I cannot even bury them, the wretched souls. All the villagers are fleeing to ancient temples on the high plateau to pray for deliverance from the Cloud. If coca fell into virtuous hands, we would bless them, but I do not think that is probable. Please, you must ask the Cloud to avoid this disaster, by protecting us and coca."

Chris placed his hand on the Mayor's shoulder to calm him, his body was vibrating with anxiety, Dear Mayor, the distribution of coca for the benefit of mankind is only a part of the Cloud's program. I am sure it is aware of the potential problems this Edict will cause."

"And in the meantime?" the mayor wasn't sure Chris understood the desperateness of his situation.

"We have been given a reprieve of twenty years to work out the program, so we must be patient." Chris' attempt failed to placate him.

"And the killing fields whose stench reaches the sky? To the Cloud!"

"Whatever, sir. The Cloud is kind. I am more hopeful than you are."

"What is our choice, our destiny depends on the will of others. We are one village, sir."

"How true, Mr. Mayor. But you must get some rest. There is much to do."

"My blood is Incan."

"I never prayed to an Incan God."

The Mayor stared straight into Chris' eyes, "I shall pray to the Cloud!"

"Prayer is prayer." Chris offered.

The mayor bowed and left without another word.

Rebel Dead

Chris chose his walking stick and donned his alpaca jacket. The sun was high and the air brisk. It was three miles downhill from the scope to the plain that abutted the jungle. The trek was hard across stubble and loose stone and ups and downs at elevation which tired him quickly. He had forgotten to take some coca before he left to counteract the slack oxygen. He spied the killing ground by a dense mass of carrion birds fighting for rights.

Then the stench of the dead closed in as he came nearer. He placed his bandan across his mouth and nose and jammed his dark glasses against his eyes for they were smarting from the vapor which issued from the jungle edge. He came upon body after body in varying stages of decay and tropical mold. He sidestepped the bodies of rebel peasants who had been stripped of meager belongings.

Where was she, the petite colonel who was so brave and dedicated to cause. He found her standing against a palisage, naked, bayoneted several times, her eyes plucked out by magpies expecting equals. The assailant had left the bayonet behind in her chest. She too had been stripped of belongings. Chris gasped at the sight. He must bury her. But with what? He had no spade, no digging utensil. He lifted her body which was rigid.

He placed the Abigail's body in the cavity which was wide enough. He mumbled an indistinct childhood prayer which he hardly remembered. He collected boulders and stones in order to block the mouth of the cave until it was a cairn.

Chris rested from time to time, the task was more than arduous. He lost his bandana and the odors surrounding him gagged him into coughing fits.

It was hours. The sun was crimson. Shadows passed over the cairn like the cerecloth over a tomb.

He stood back satisfied with his work. It was a fitting burial, except for taps, for the little American colonel, Abigail Simpson.

The Top

Back at the scope, unshowered dressed only in long underwear, Chris had a chew of coca and trained the scope on the moon which was full and low on the horizon. His shirt vermillion stained in bloody hues. Yes, like a moonstone. There was no sign of the Cloud. Did it know what he had done. Did it approve?

The dogs and lamas had been killed. Troops savored meat of any kind after months in the jungle of scarce and uncertain game. Chris learned federal troops did not approve of the spying scope. The commander feared a landslide. It was possible considering the outcropping half way up the peak. Scavenging, they ransacked the huts, rummaged to the end of everything that stood and burned. The mayor was a prisoner.

What was there to do now? The death of the petite colonel was on his mind, persistent. What was going on elsewhere was known to him through his radio and computer.

The Andes! He had flown over mountain ranges, the Alps, on the fringe of the Himalayas, the Rocky Mountains, the Sierra Nevada, and the Appalachians. There was never more absorbing a flight that a small plane over the Andes. How different another view above ancient cities moldering on plateaus, crumbling terraces and traces of tipsy water ways and irrigation to catch glacial water, and mist. Yet there was still life below, the herds of lamas, sheep, native villagers, and the hardy inhabitants. The Andes bore the color of a brownish gold streaked with silver as if reflecting the mining treasures in its rocks. The sunsets too, were burnished, not spectacular but elegant in deep hues. As, as he flew closer to the ground with the light Piper, large patches of green vegetation sprouted, which he guessed to be coca.

Peaks rose in titanic totemic sculptures. The rain was corrosive and leveled palaces of kings. Thunder was dulled by the spaciousness of the range. And the silence, a whisper of ancient tongues and rituals.

The meteors were short lived, scintillating as they crossed his watch. The Milky Way shown a silver brooch above his head. The wind, cold and frigid whirled the mist in showy shrouds, rock slides roared.

Days and night were vibrant with beauty and beauty was a nice emotion. The only creature on earth that recognized beauty and was capable of ecstasy in its presence was man. That was a given. With beauty came passion. There was no passion in the Andes, fundamentally it was a cruel place, a diamond bracelet on a pillow gives no comfort to sleepless nights.

Chris gave these matters much thought as he groomed Luis who mumbled no response. He too, needed companionship, the soothing of ruffled feather, and the assurance of love with a nip. He pinched himself to be humble. From his height, he sometimes felt godlike, removed from humanity, divine, and in his divinity, he pinched himself again.

Condor Flight

What was the future? Waiting the span of twenty years? He, the parrot and the scope. The Cloud had used his living voice as the vehicle for a message. Was he not a kind messenger? As such, what would he be doing in his isolation on the Andes Peak? A message to whom? To a palpable silence which did not respond? Where was his audience amid the howling eddies of the winds? He was no prophet who coveted sloughs. He was one who would head for the plains among the self damning humans like himself. He vowed to himself that he would not assume he would be a reminder of the presence of the Cloud and it demands.

Before he could leave his isolation he must learn what was happening in the plains of the earth, in the towns, villages, giant cities. What was his kind up to? How were they behaving? What progress? For two weeks, his ears were glued to the radio, his eyes on the internet. He gathered all the information available to him, what he saw was encouraging and discouraging. There was worldwide legislation to criminalize abortion. Tired and jaded incumbents were being revoked by younger men. Pornography was under siege everywhere. the offer of free cocaine to billions a thorn in the flesh.

He was waiting for instruction. The Cloud was no help. He read and reread the demands as a breviary. Raw reality moved Chris to hours of despair as he chewed his coca, and chatted with Luis. Surfing the various search engines, he came upon an article from a magazine reporter who traveled in Mexico recently that gave him an unplanted picture of what was happening in the thousands of villages in Mexico, Bolivia, Columbia and Peru. The reporter detected militancy in the cartels and rebels for better systems of justice and governance. In many places, these groups had established their own sovereignties and ruled, some thought justly, and widely as second government. To which did he belong in time and place.

Exacerbating, arching worldwide problem, the trafficking and commerce in drugs, especially cocaine. Although sovereign nations were in agreement about eliminating illicit drugs and regularizing the administration of cocaine to the world's population there existed parcels and sub government of innumerable cartel of drug lords, rebels, bankers, crooked politicians and corrupt police who moved against any addict to curtail control over coca and drugs. It was protocol half the world now. A moral potency to undermine, and crush the cocaine rejuvenation despite any threat of extinction. In the short term, profits, money and the devil take the hind most.

So, its all about profit and money. There a keening of a yearning for social justice Chris thought hard. Was this a clunk of armor, could this militancy for power or profit be turned around under the guidance of the advice of the Cloud? Who was to remind these cartels and rebels of the underlying purpose of their militancy, substantial purpose of their purposes. How for us to remind them? A reminder, who, why, Chris himself? For an instance, he mocked himself. He, the reminder? He winced at the idea. Then, it settled in his mind more consciously. Why not the spokesman for the Cloud. It was his voice which spoke. He was fit, he thought.

So Christopher Christopherson made his preparation. "Messenger!" He shut down the mechanism of the scope, provided a pole to carry the parrot, gathered his clothing into a battered duffle. He looked at himself in a tall mirror. He had lost ten pounds, his hair had grayed down the nape of his neck, his eyes were wrinkled but still steely grey, his face had narrowed. He had lost a side tooth, his lips were full, his expression not brave or apprehensive, but determined. In his inner pocket in a roll, he slipped his copy of the text of the Cloud and the diary and last letter of Abigail Simpson.

The morning was bright, the snows melting and migratory birds overhead. The road down to the plain was hard stubble and stony stone. He laced his hiking boots and shouldered his light carbine rifle. Devastation had turned farmers into bandits and the rebels and Federales were still roaming the countryside.

Chris started the jeep provided by the Institute on the third try. The jeep is a prize possession, he was sure of that. He stored twenty gallons of gas in the back, and took a last farewell look at the Andes.

Their silence will forever hum in his hearing. The memory of its totemic glyphs, the three dimensional view of ancient cities ensconced in its declivities, the abandoned outline of fertile terraces of extinct crops and coca, the crude temple steps vine choked and mossy, the silver pall of glacial streams, the imperial flight of red condors, and the overall vision of worn gold.

He gave a salute in the direction of the cairn of the little colonel, revved the jeep, a farewell under his breath. He was now the peregrinating witness of the Cloud's appearance.

The Federales Major

Fifty miles from the scope at the foot hills, he was halted by a blockade of Federales. They asked no questions, but guided him to the Commandant's tent staffed with flags. The federal soldiers and officers were smart in red uniforms and new arms. A corpulent woman sergeant shoved Chris forward into the tent where he faced the Commandant, a major, clean shaven, completely bald with hollowed eyes, a martinet mustache and an impish beard in triangular cut. His English was border perfect. He had Chris' passport in his hand.

"Christopherson," he said, "the astronomer at the observatory."

"I am sir."

"Are you leaving?"

"We had orders not to disturb you."

"It is time to move."

"Where is it you are moving to? May I ask?"

"I have been too long alone."

"With your parrot?" the Major smiled wrily.

"Sort of. Sort of." Chris replied.

"A beautiful bird. Does he talk?"

"A word or two." Chris wondered where the Major was going with this.

"Not much conversation, then? So, you ran out of stars and here I was taught there are millions out there who can talk as well as the parrot." The major was playing with words.

"Don't sir me so abjectly, Mr. Christopherson. You are an eminent personage. We have universities and are host to the observatory."

"I was subject to them."

"Then you will be obedient."

"In what sense?" Chris was impatient with this banter.

"You will tell me about the rebels who passed your ways months ago."

"Yes, I spoke to a Colonel. And she was leading her company to an encounter with you."

"Do you know if she is dead?"

"So, I heard."

"And from whom did you hear this?"

"Scavenging natives." Chris lied.

"Are you sure of this?" the Major tilted his head and stared back at Chris.

"I believed them. I saw no one returning alive."

The Major wiped his nose with a lace handkerchief. "My scouts have told me so. We ambushed them all. Did you have to be told? You had the scope."

Where was the Major going with this dance, Chris wondered almost aloud.

"Did you give any intelligence to your American compatriot?"

"I would not say compatriot. I shared nothing with her but the face that were both American."

"Americanos, si! When one has a telescope of that magnitude it enables you to see what is going on anywhere, eh?"

"It has limitations, Major."

"It has limitations."

"But you are the discoverer of the asteroid, the Cloud!"

"After many years."

"You are a distinguished man. We want you on our side."

"I take no sides, Major. I know nothing of your argument. I am as neutral and uninvolved as a neutron star."

"Our President has cooperated fully with the States in curbing drug traffic. It is counterproductive to have an American citizen take arms against a lawful sovereignty that it doing its best." He said emphatically.

Chris took his time in answering, "I have heard good things about your President and his cooperative."

"I am glad to have met you, Mr. Christopherson. You have assured me that the mischievous colonel is dead so that I can properly notify my government who will relay the information to Washington. What we would like to do is warn misguided radicals not to volunteer for enlistment with rebels. We need no martyrs. The drug wars are destroying Latin and South America. You say you are a neutron star, but one has sympathies such as the use of coca. My men found a stash in your jeep," a snide smile spread across the Major's lips.

"I use it carefully, prescribed." Why was he defending himself in this context. He laughed inwardly at the absurdity of it all.

"Sir, scientist, with all respect, coca is such a dirty habit. Imagine what would happen to my mustache if I indulged!" he primped his mustache with a pointed index finger. "However, I shall not confiscate the coca. You may keep it and your rifle."

"I am not an addict!" Chris was weary of his game.

"Not now, Mr. Neutron Star but given safe. Don't mind the headless corpses along the way. We pay in kind. They are rebels after all. Oh, and I am keeping your parrot. Considerate it a spoil of war."

Chris was incredulous, the Major was toying with him from every angle, "I am not at war with anyone."

The major ignored his comment, "Perhaps I shall teach him to say, "Viva Coca! Si!"

Rebel Veterinarian

Chris slipped into the jeep without the company of his parrot. He drove on checking his diminishing gasoline. Downhill for three days, his route was unobstructed. On the outskirts, he was hailed by a patrol of rebels and escorted to a looted police station. He was led to wait in a dirty bathroom that stunk of feces. Then, after hours, he was dragged into the presence of the rebel chief sitting behind a pitted table, smoking a long cheroot. He was a tall man his legs spanned the width of the table. He was using a Federales helmet as a spittoon, he spat often, with a mouth of perfect teeth.

"I have been waiting for you, Mr. Christopherson." He pushed a bottle of tequila to Chris' side across the table, but there were no glasses. "Drink! We rebels share everything with no care for teapot ceremony. I know you have met the Federals who probably offered you no tequila, stingy like the government."

"They were courteous. " Chris replied curtly.

"But they took your parrot!" He shook his head. "They commanded the hopes of the people so what is a parrot."

"He meant much to me."

"It does you credit Senor, I fancy all animals but the Federales. Tell me where are you heading?

"To Mexico."

"Why Mexico, Senor?"

"I have been isolated at the observatory for some time and I am curious of what is happening."

"You are not a wanderer on earth as an astronomer. You have been cooped up and you have wandered among the stars, Senor," he straightened in his seat, "I am a university man myself, by profession a veterinarian. I would have examined your parrot free of charge."

"Thank you, Captain."

"So, you are leaving us and the observatory? Our observatory has made history recently. That business about that cloud," he waved his hand dismissively. "Now, that is poppycock, probably static electricity or extreme hackers have dominated the waves, or a canyon reverberation, an old broadcast by kooks. You are an astrophysicist, you surely don't believe in any message?"

"I am curious Senor, I await results."

The Captain stood up, stretched and walked to the bulky shutters and stared out the window, "We too await results. Results of six years of war against the Federales, against the government corrupt as Hades," he shot Chris a look over his shoulder. "Our rebellion, if you call it that, is a persuasion, at least, that is how it began. The poor are poorer than they were a hundred years ago. The government has colluded with the drug traffickers for years, every police command and politician has profited. We are back to the days of Pancho Villa and Zapata, but with drug trafficking money to support our program. We have used a great part of the drug money for clinics, hospitals, schools, orphanages. We have even tried to make the farmers prosper, although it was drugs providing the fund for reclamation. So in this schizoid situation coca is naturally beneficial. The notion of the Cloud in regard to the largesse of coca is a jejune notion, impractical and dangerous. But we do not argue with the Cloud if it professes to be with us. Most of the world does not understand our predicament. We are not customers of arm's merchants with loads of credit and financing by speculators. We literally beg for arms from sympathizers, capture those of the Federales, and jerry build our own. Of course, we don't hope to win this battle, if you want to call it that, this revolution. We hope for a stalemate, some miracle which will be a topsy turvy for a new era, a new man," he turned to face Chris squarely.

"I know the psychology of animals, horses, dogs, parrots, mules, but the psychology of man is egotistical, reckless and selfish. Self individuation has become an excuse for the exploitation of others. It has become a dangerous shibboleth that excuses all individual caprice and depredation upon the rest of human kind. Look around! You ask, how is it to be accomplished, lions will sleep with the lamb? Look! See the shedding of blood, headless corpses, the death of the little Colonel--we know about that, too. No proclamation for a wayward boulder or star cluster will orchestrate the beginning of new man."

Chris inhaled his cigar thoughtfully. "You are very eloquent, Captain."

"Mexico? You will see from a distance a beautiful land ravaged for centuries by revolution. A scrubby golf course, no orchids, stripped trees, yellow vegetables, plowed coca and marijuana and deserts of brown sand. It is not fruitful, all blood soaked vintages."

"Then I am free to go?"

"Of course, and, may I have your autograph before you leave? I will guarantee your safety from rebels for the remainder of your journey. But wait, Senor Scientist, I have a surprise for you! My council has authorized me to make available to you a helicopter on the premises. It can carry you close to the border."

Chris' eyes could not hide his confusion, "Thank your council for me."

"By the way, if the Cloud's tribunal needs a veterinarian, I am at your service," he smiled broadly and laughed loudly.

Chris was so overwhelmed by the whole affair with the Captain, that he could only bow as he exited, then walked backwards through the door with slow steps.

Playing Field of Coca

Instead of the border, he was flown to the outskirts of Mexico City, landing at an airfield controlled by the provincial rebels. He was vetted at every stop along the way. He was now in the sway of the American Council of Mexico City who greeted him effusively and offered assistance. Yes, Chris told him, he needed money and a vehicle. The Council gladly and willingly gave him a staff Ford to resume his return to the States. He also needed a change of clothing. He pretended nothing illegal in his possession.

So from this congenial welcome of the fellow American, Chris began what was to become a many year jaunt to tell his fellowman what he had learned about the asteroid. He was no apostle in the crude sense of the word. He had been a witness as others but no one had shared the same ground of space with an elusive object who demands were upsetting the known world.

He appeared in forums and lectures where there were huzzahs, objections to his presence and to the message of the Cloud. Fearful of assassination four FBI men had been assigned to protect him. He shunned them, dismissed them.

The devout kissed his hands or his boots, but he was never mobbed. In general he was listened too. He made no attempt at rhetoric, or effects. He gave a straight forward account of his

52

discovery of the sky object and the monitoring of it for years at different observatories around the world and the involuntary preemption of his voice by the Cloud to proclaim the conditions of probation and reprieve. He needed no lecture agent for a tour, personally accepting invitations to seminars and congresses.

In Mexico City, he found much greater acceptance and welcome in the frightened populace of ten million souls than he did among his confreres in the astrophysics community, who were of two minds about his professional integrity. Many of them were scoffed at the hokum surrounding the Cloud. Some belittled this mystical message from a hitherto a mute void. The hypothesis that unborn children were to advise the world on geopolitics, economy, science and social justice was arrogant. Many prominent and equally famous thought Chris was delusional, off, a renegade scientist. An article in the Astrophysics journal opined that it was a wonder the children did not pee on the world. Ah!

Maddalena

addalena Vasquez presented herself with a solid kick on his door which opened it ajar slamming it against the wall. The introduction was very dramatic, apt of the mannish young women who now faced him in a wide legged stance to challenge, which appeared to be her intention.

Chris stood up to greet her when she said commandingly, "Sit down, Senor." Puzzled he sought a chair and sat down.

"We must talk," she said.

Now annoyed with the handsome woman who stood astride in his doorway, he said, "Then close the door."

She did and moved closer to him. He saw her better now, in her mid twenties, wheat blond hair in strict braids like military rolls, an aquiline face with wide eyes in mascara, a narrow nose that could be shorter, tall and shapely in designer denims, short linen blouse and black boots. Her voice had a contralto timbre. Who was she this intemperate woman who kicks shut doors?

"I am Maddalena Vasquez," she announced as she closed the door and sat across from on the small sofa. "I am a freelance reporter for the New York Times."

"I imagine you have credentials, why can't you knock?"

"Because, Mr. Christopherson, I want you to know where I am coming from."

"I am familiar with some of your dispatches." Chris responded with annoyance. "And where is that?"

"They say I am a buster, the La Familia does not like me, the Federales despise me, and the evangelicals abhor me. I don't expect much else from you." she stared directly at him.

Chris shook his head, where was she going with this, "I hardly know you."

"You are a charlatan scientist, the cartel will either kill you or use you and the crazy evangelicals will crucify you," Maddalena said with an air of certainty.

"Have you come to insult me or to save me from an imminent fate?"

"I report what I see to be the truth, but the rewrite man obliterates my thought."

And your thought, is? I am listening." To Chris her passion for an uncertain cause was subliminally fervent. What cause, he wondered.

"I am a thorough skeptic of everything that has been done to curb the drug traffic and bring some sanity to millions of Mexicans, Bolivians, Peruvians, actually most of Latin and South America. Psychologies are crippled, hypocrisies abound in the world, respectable banks and pillars of society are laundering more than fifty billion dollars a year, enough to buy the economy of Spain or Portugal. You stop laundering you stop the cartels' powers. Corruption is any word for representative government, all the incumbents are thieves and looters." She was breathless.

"And you are not a rebel?" Chris said

She pulled at her hair, a smoldering anger ebbing. "I am in a way, against my father. I am half Sicilian. My father came here years ago to profit from the drug trade with Europe. He is now dead. He abandoned me and my mother for whores, I hated him. And I hate all things connected with crime!" She clenched and unclenched her hands. "Perhaps this will sound sophomoric, but I yearn for truth, for transparency. Say that I am an idealist who's disappointed in the lack of ideals, or the suggestion of any. My father sent me to the best schools, he had no son. I graduated from the London School of Economics. Let me be frank. I am what they call an iconoclast. And that is why I oppose you and the rest of your misguided gooders."

"You misunderstand me, Ms Vasquez, I too am a reporter." Chris was not sure he should be defending himself to her.

"But your reporting says nothing of your feelings." She shook her head in reprimand.

"I only report what I have seen with the eyes of a scientist. I became a foisted mouthpiece for a phenomenon for which I did not volunteer. My role is as spokesman in intimate contact with the asteroid, the Cloud. I do not deny what I saw. If the world is forgetting that unusual experience then I am here to remind them that it did appear. I have a responsibility to science. We may all be mistaken about the importance of the Cloud, the asteroid, only time will tell. Twenty years will tell. I am open minded and hopeful. I don't see like you what can untangle this skein of misguided motives, good or bad, rebels, revolutionaries, new bibles, preaching from the many. We must be patient and wait on events and encourage some compliance with the edicts of the asteroid." Chris was being as straight with her as he could be.

"There you go with your mumbo jumbo again," she snorted.

"What did you make of the asteroid?" he asked.

"As a born skeptic, the event goes against my grain, however, there are moments when my mother's rosary, which I still have gives me second thoughts," her voice muted.

"What does the Times think of me, really?"

"They are puzzled, reserved." Maddalena was hedging. "They are concerned about their own fate and editorial policy. They know they must eventually take a stand endorsing the revelation of the asteroid or destroy it. It's their ass. Everyone is gambling, all at risk of making a misjudgment or lack of faith of a supernatural event."

"It is not easy, I know." He responded solemnly.

"I think you need protection, Mr. Christopherson, and that is why I am here. I have dealt with the rebels, revolutionaries and cartels. I will tell them of your intentions and that you are not a threat, but just possibly a revisionist of their own political philosophies. I believe if I can vouchsafe for you they will not kill you."

Chris smiled, "I see you have already become fond of me."

Chris reached into his computer case for Abigail Simpson's journals. "I was given this for safe keeping by a young American female, an Amherst grad who volunteered for service to the poor in Bolivia, who ultimately joined the rebel army. She came to see me at the Bolivian observatory. She and the last of a local rebel group were bivouacked in the surrounding hills. She died in battle shortly after. There are many entries, read them, you may want to print some excerpts."

He had mailed the letter to her mother and sister months ago. That was a personal matter, not a news item.

A Fatal Visit

It was early morning when he opened his eyes. He blinked, someone was sitting patiently beside his bed. He sat upright.

"Good Morning, Senor Scientist." The veterinarian was instantly voluble.

"Goodness," mumbled Chris.

"Yes, yes, I have come to congratulate you!"

"You?" Chris exclaimed.

"I have often thought about you." He waved a broad hand in the air.

"And I you."

The rebel captain took two cheroots from his vest pocket and handed one to Chris. "It must be a long time since you smoked our cheroots, I'll lift it for you," which he did.

Chris gave it a starting puff.

"Senor Scientist, I am in mufti." He passed his hands over his styled suit and glossy jodhpurs.

"You did not come to Mexico City to do shopping." Chris said drily.

"To my friend, at last after five years in the jungle I am on a kind of holiday."

"Such as," Chris inquired.

"I am a deputy of the rebel council, perhaps of all rebels throughout the world, basically we are all revolutionaries. We are conjuring on joining force to encourage a social and moral evolution. I often think back on the summary court presided over by the animals, especially the dogs. They too will be pleased."

"Dear Veterinarian, I am glad to taste a cheroot again, to clasp your hand and thank the council for the helicopter. I am hopeful, as you are and share your optimism, but it is premature, we still have years ahead of us to earn our reprieve."

"Senor Chris, dear mentor, I get nightmares imagining that the Cloud is a mere fiction, a hallucination, an erratic echo of a crazed evangelist. Tell me it is not so, that you are convinced body and soul that the Cloud is real and a rebel?"

"Friend, what can I say? Proof? I am a pariah in the eyes of many and subject to much ridicule. That is my nightmare, but I shake it off as we do with all bad dreams and rise to a sunny day. I am willing to wait out the term of probation.

Fate of Coca

Chris was busy answering emails when he heard a passkey in the door of his hotel apartment. The door opened and a massive man appeared in ill fitting street clothes. He bowed to Chris and closed the door behind him.

"Good Day, Senor."

"Good Day?" Chris wondered.

"Excuse my abrupt entrance, but I don't always find doors locked in mid afternoon. A precaution perhaps," he said with diamond studded teeth.

"No precaution, Senor, one naps sometimes and does not wish to be disturbed." Chris quipped back.

"Maddalena Vasquez is very concerned about you and that is why I am here, Guillermo Luis at your service." The man bowed slightly.

"Maddalena?"

"Yes, Maddalena. I am deputy commander of all the cartels. I presided over a sit-down regarding you only yesterday, to decide your fate, Senor Christopherson," he helped himself to a chair which hardly fit his bulk. His head was small, his lips always pursed as if thinking aloud. His hands were huge and hairy.

Chris turned off his computer, got up from the desk, walked to the window, and stared down into the avenue below. In a low voice he turned to his visitor, "And the verdict?"

The deputy raised his fist in the palm of his left hand. "Neutral, Senor, for the moment. As a confrere of yours said, Senor, you are 'a neutral star.' He, along with the veterinarian and Maddalena Vasquez pleaded your case. General opinion was that you are a threat to our mission."

"Me, I am not a threat." Chris was weary of this posturing already.

"Don't be ingenious, Senor. Maddalena has told us that you have an acute intelligence and an ear for conspiracies, local or worldwide. And although we may disagree with certain points of view, we respect you as a distinguished astronomer."

"That is something, I suppose."

"Maddalena knows my thoughts on many things." Chris volunteered.

"She explained them eloquently to the council, so eloquent in fact we could not distinguish her judgment about you from her fondness for you. She made a great case for you, factual and emotional, so you are not by any means this 'neutral star,'" he rolled his eyes as if to punctuate his statement. "I am not a ladies' man, Senor, but let us say she has a deep regard for you as a man and a scientist.

Chris appeared confused and embarrassed. He walked back and sat down to face his caller.

"Excuse me, Senor, I was a bit flip. I am afraid perhaps I have alarmed you who had no deep regard of love." He retorted.

"O ! Come now, deputy, what are those words. I am only an observer, if asked, that is all. I have deep respect for Maddalena and I thank her for her advocacy and plea for my life. Why did she succeed?"

Her father, Michele, was for years our representative in Europe, and here too. He was a fine and honorable Mafioso who did good service with us for years. We did not hesitate to respect his memory by patience with an impetuous daughter who could be in love with you. We respect that, love, so for now our stance is neutral, wait and see."

"Where is Maddalena now?" Chris asked.

"I suspect she is at the door, listening. Shall I open it?"

"No, no," Chris pondered a moment. "No harm must come to her because of me. I could never forgive myself if something happened to her. If I am a neutral star, so is she."

"Senor Christopherson you have become an expert during your stay in the Andes. You have shown signs of sympathy with our cause or the opposition. Neutral? A scientist obsessed with that asteroid which many colleagues say was a giant mirage and not a true revelation."

Chris responded defensively as he had so many times before, "I have always said it was a phenomenon unexplained."

"If those edicts of the asteroid come to fruition, it means extinction!"

"Or change, or vindication."

"Senor, you hold out hope for us." He seemed sincere.

"We must believe the warnings of the Cloud. If it was a mirage what was the source of the mirage. How did it originate? What was the simulacrum?"

"Of course, I do not understand half of what you are saying, however, you are no mirage but flesh and blood with whom a fine woman is in love in the midst of a perilous situation. Love is no mirage."

"True, true, Senor." Chris wondered.

"Buenos Dias," the big man rose to his feet and walked slowly towards the door and opened it carefully.

"Buenos Dias, Senor Luis. Please don't trip over Maddalena if she is behind the door."

Double Stars

addalena crept into the room in the wake of the Guillermo Luis' departure. She grinned sheepishly at Chris,

"Maddalena, you heard everything like a serving maid at the door?"

"Yes!" she murmured with eyes downcast.

"So what he said is true, you plead for my life at the sit down council?"

"It is divinely true." She confessed openly. "it was one of your finest moments."

"If they finally incriminate me, they will harm you."

She edged closer to him, knelt at the foot of his chair, grouped the strands of her loose blond hair, rearranged her skirt, put her palms together prayerfully in confession, pushed her mouth sorrowfully and said, "I prayed openly for your life." She leaned on his bronzed arm, "the council was prepared to order your execution."

"I cannot believe this. Why? I am not threat to man."

"They trust only their own fanaticism. If I weren't half Mafiso they would never tolerate me."

""He spoke of love. That you love me." Chris looked down on her face.

"Oh, you don't understand the Spaniards. Talk of love creates affability, amiability and gossipy interest. It pleases the palate of Spanish machismo and make my pleas more logical for a woman-a kind of reverse gallantry." Maddalena said tossing her head back.

Perhaps relieved, he said. "Then you don't love me?"

"But I do, I do!" she shouted.

"You do?" Chris blinked rapidly.

"Yes, you see, I half love you."

"Half love?" Chris scratched his head and shook it from side to side.

"Yes, I half love myself and I half love you."

Chris pulled on his nose in disbelief. "What a day! Maddalena, what," he cried out exasperatedly and sighed deeply.

"It is perfectly clear, if you will only listen," she raised her right hand. "See this loves you," and then she raised her left hand, "and this loves me." She was more emotional than he had ever seen her, "Don't you see, in your parlance, it is a double star, one's radiance shines upon the other as they traipse through space."

Chris pretended to tear out his hair in concentration. "Neutral star! Double star, what is this? a parody of my profession?"

Maddalena was right back at him," It is a beautiful parallelism of the star. I thought it was a very romantic conception."

Chris stood up and went to the window.

"I am not a feminist, Chris, but I like to think like a man, romantic love is selfish love. I want my love to irradiate you and still remain lambent myself. I must love myself to love you. Double stars irradiating each other. I must honor myself as you must honor yourself with no cheap pillow talk."

"How elevated your talk is, Maddalena." Chris turned to stare at her still kneeling.

"Because you elevate my thoughts --that double star, Christopher! A poet said poetry is universal, that it exists in everyone—that it is an ingredient of the soul—that it is on the breath of the new born.

The children in the Cloud know that foremost is love that knows itself, but wishes to be expressed through kindness and collective well being. To love something is to know It."

"You are very profound, Maddalena."

"The children in the Cloud know that love is not totally expressed as it must be, it is latent and lame. The children's hearts tell them out of consummate pity of their own fate, that love must be expressed universally by all peoples of the world in whatever language or gesture, in order to bring about a better world, not a Utopia, but a general feeling of love and well being and the beneficial results will follow as night the day." Maddalena paused for a deep breath, then, continued, "You are a noble person, Chris. I know that is an old fashioned word, but it will do here. You are the spokesman for that Cloud, you have been chosen for good reasons. You are a believer in the Cloud. You love them or they would not love you in return. I know I must be worthy of you, share you, my double star."

"And?" Chris asked in soft voice.

"As for the rest, I am not sure." Maddalena reflected for several moments, "but I am sure of one thing."

"And that is?

"Are you fond of poetry."

"Yes, very.

"Then you see the double star."

"Oh, Maddalena, love and poetry?" Chris ran his fingers through his hair.

"Why not?" she asked.

"Maddalena, Maddalena, we are in the midst of a moral maelstrom, headless bodies everywhere, rebels, revolutionaries, crackpots, wholesale slaughter, violation of every human right and," she interrupted him mid sentence, "And that is why the Cloud appeared, a children's crusade and perhaps that will shut your sardonic mouth." She instantly tried to withdraw the sharp statement but Chris had tweaked her nose.

"Maddalena, as a partner star I am beginning to feel my nearness to you."

"Intimately?"

O, woman, I am fifteen years older than you."

"You misunderstand me, I mean intimately, not sexually, although my libido is fine and I have had my share of young lovers, but I never loved anyone halfway, but you."

Chris smiled wrily, "A double star never wins, Maddalena, it's not nature."

Maddalena rose to her full height and stared straight into Chris' face, "Chris, I detest home sweet home domesticity and wish myself dear as mere wife. I want to be your double star."

A Daughter's Defection

C hris could almost be her father. Strangely, the relationship was not of lovers of a miss marriage. Even though she was young, she was his intellectual equal. She was a vitalist and he felt worn and used in comparison. Sex was a necessary function and his act suffused with tenderness. Not sex, but a sexless affection. Such brightness and affection gave him joy. For an aging man, he held her close in a glow of coca.

For Chris, the rebels intermixed in person and flimsy creeds. The inanition of jungle warfare and bombings and massacres gave them the cachet of criminals. This was the confusion in his mind when he met the Federales and the rebels of a half dozen factions in undistinguished uniforms. That so called revolution of Oliviero's was now a fiction, a headless belief as feckless as those heads on the roads. Death stilled all arguments.

Maddalena! Only her reports insensibly called for a trumpet call to reason and agreement. Her intensity and productivity became ever more noticeable to the the Barons of drugs and mayhem. And what was that call to arms or to sanity? Her cry was for a cease fire on all fronts, a return to comity of well meaning brothers.

Maddalena bunked with Chris at the hotel. He rented an adjoining room for her needs, a bed, a desk and a wide view of the square below. The nights were long when he was lecturing in the States. Chris longed for her between her dispatches to the New York Times every Wednesday. And so, the double stars often merged and then became distant again. He in his room she in hers.

They were not secluded by any means, below was the square where there were many demonstrations defying the tenets of the Cloud and pilgrimages of penitence for the coming accounting. Vast movements of people were moving across the face of the earth. The privileged fought for position and profit but the swelling underclass became believers of the Cloud and its purpose.

This powerful movement which had already reinforced the will of police and the Federals to prosecute the cartels and throw out corrupt incumbents was not due to Chris' scholarly lectures or to the appeal of the Cloud's verdict. It was due to the tremendous import of Maddalena's dispatches to the Times and the world. Every day edged in favor for the Cloud. There was counter publicity and the favorite theme that the Cloud was another fantastical Children's Crusade and similarly doomed to abysmal failure. It was derided with much force. Huge parades of ridicule were occurring on city streets. Protesters wheeled baby strollers and incubators, hoisted bannered diapers festooned with pink and blue ribbons and nipples. They sang songs about baby faced and naughty children.

They scoffed, were grownups to be ruled by sniffling infants and that tribunal of beasts. How absurd it all was. And yet the movement of repentance moved like a riptide crossing all beliefs and shattering any secure moment of security.

Maddalena reported all in incautious missives that reached a global audience. She chronicled the state of affairs as she saw them. The cartels were in disarray facing non cooperation in activities and money laundering. The Federales had become increasingly effective in Mexico, Peru and Bolivia acting in concert with the US DEA. Sects were claiming the trafficking of coca in God's name. Her dispatches became longer and longer and even more widely syndicated. She began to editorialize, showing her true colors, which the Council of cartels recognized as treachery.

When Maddalena convinced the Times to publish extracts from the journals of Abigail Simpson, it created a sensation with consequences. The mass media played up Abigail Simpson as a crusading impressionable nudnik who believed her liberal professors. Her image was splashed across computer screens as a jungle fighter. Her family was hemmed with reporter's who stole her photographs to reproduce on sheets and film. Incidents were fabricated about Abigail's exploits during her time in South America. Ultimately, all mounted to propaganda and publicity that alarmed the revolutionaries and rebels. They inflamed the Council.

Likewise, Maddalena Vasquez was hailed as an intrepid journalist eligible for a Pulitzer Prize.

She knew she had made many enemies, but did not seem to care. She had made it her crusade. Chris had warned her of the imminent danger but she waved off his pleas for caution. Rumor had it that the council was of one opinion and decision. What decision? Chris sensed they were being followed. He knew there was a price to pay for her betrayal regardless of the past power of her father. He heard her on a phone interview in the next room. He had made up his mind to take her on a flight for safety, but where? The Jungle, Canada?

The next evening there was a planned demonstration in the square below their hotel with signs declaring that Maddalena Vasquez was a danger to a new democracy of the evangelicals and the cartels. She was a traitor spying for foreign interests, for the status quo, that she was anathema to progress and a conspirator in the conjuring of false mirages such as the Cloud.

Chris still wore the magical cloak of a distinguished American scientist and citizen but she was out there alone in the killing field without the protecting arm of her father.

How could she be so oblivious to the danger to herself. She behaved like an inspired apostle of the Cloud.

With each passing day Chris was becoming more hysterical and convinced she was marked for death. How and when? They were double stars. He stared at her in the adjoining room. There she was with her fingers flying across her computer keyboard. She was content at her desk like a sparrow on a branch ready to be shot down.

Chris barged into her room, his eyes wide and darting. "Maddalena get packed."

"What has gotten into you, Christopher." she had never seen him like this.

"Maddalena, is it only a matter of time, you are condemned. I am convinced of that. We must run, run, now!" his words and breath came in short bursts.

"Sit down and collect yourself." She took both his hands in hers.

"Don't you understand, you no longer have my immunity! We must leave! I still have the jeep. It is loaded with gas, we will head for western Canada. They will never find you there."

She held a sheet of paper in her hand. "Chris, my darling, I have just resigned, or better the Times has fired me. So, I am out of danger, there you see?" she handed him the copy of the email she had just relayed.

"It is too late, that will not matter now, the hard truth in the council's eyes is that you are a traitor and must be punished."

"How do you know I am marked?" she asked.

"Don't you remember I am a double star. It feel it, I feel your danger." Chris knelt beside her and held her face in his hands. "I beg you as I love you, Maddalena, come, come with me, now. I share your fate. I must for I love you."

She patted his head. "Love, love, we were thinking of a greater love."

"That can wait for twenty years from now. Your life is now, now, any moment, I feel it, and if we don't act quickly I shall be paralyzed in your behalf." Chris was shaking.

"Chris, I do feel your fear and concern. I'll go with you, but I must pack and change into some rough clothing for the journey. Do you still have your rifle?

"It's in the jeep. Hurry!"

Celebratory shots were heard outside the window. Had news of Maddalena's resignation hit the streets already?

Chris collected his dark glasses, a large brimmed hat and his alpaca jacket. He pulled on a pair of hardened boots. The jungle would provide no refuge? No, they could never go South. They would head North and seek asylum somehow at the consulate in Canada.

Maddalena packed a large duffle and her computer case, and stood at his doorway in less than twenty minutes. "I am ready."

There was no obstacle to their leaving. They took the staircase down two floors, the lobby was empty and the demonstration had subsided. The way was clear to his jeep parked in a nearby shanty garage. Good! The cover was shielding them against a strong late afternoon sun. It was only two hours before nightfall. They would be on the road under cover of dark, free from surveillance. Chris calculated that they could reach the US border after a night's layover in the jeep. The garage attendant accepted a tip and asked no questions. No one did. No one was around. Were his fears real? Exaggerated. He did not think so. The air was full of acid smoke from the methane factories.

Chris pulled away slowly without fuss and they were on their way. The road ahead was clear as far as he could see. They passed Federal outposts gingerly but they were not stopped for questioning. After several hours the road began to wind to bushier country with no outposts of the Federals although there were headless corpses as a warning to the peasants. They transversed an oven baked country with lime trees and spikes of argives beside the rimmed roads. But their journey was so far unimpeded. The jeep hummed well, it was suddenly dark, a moonless eve. Chris pulled the jeep between two lime trees for the night. In his rush, he had forgotten to take food along, but he did have bottles of water stored in the jeep.

They drank some water, had a snort of cocaine to delay any pangs of hunger and fell asleep in each other's arms, wrapped in native blankets to ward off the chill and the insects.

All night long they were restless in the cramped Jeep. At midnight, the moon appeared full and bright, revealing, before astonished eyes, that the jeep was parked in the midst of a coca plantation. They could see acres of coca plants blooming with white flowers like topped candles in the semi darkness. No real fragrance from the blooms, the coca had little fragrance, but it did have a penetrating scent. In a coca field there was no cocaine effect at all. What both felt was an aliveness, a potency of poison and palliative. A message that is close to the blood of humans. What was the addiction to brain and the soul? What intermingled in evolution? To Chris coca was a living thing not just a plant. The coca was alive, it was energy, it was peace. There was no somnolence. They were both wide awake staring at the acres of coca. They had no yearning for the coca that was at hand distance. No need to chew a leaf. A carpet of coca, a dream, they were aware of power.

The morning was equally quiet with little sun. They rinsed their faces with drinking water. Chris tested the tires before he started the jeep.

"Let's get on the road, Maddalena. In ten hours we shall we shall cross the border into California. And, let me warn you, my dear, when we are safe, I am going to lock you in a vault with no computer."

Coca Execution

And so they drove for several hours before they were stopped by rebel traffickers. One could tell from the garish uniforms with flamboyant red trimmings that there was no rank among the soldiers who waved them down. They had run into a rebel outpost strategic to contain the border in their favor. One small man took charge, ordered them from the jeep, claimed Chris' rifle and joined Christopher and Maddalena side by side surrounded by four armed men. No questions. There was almost an apathetic loss of attention. Chris suspected that they were drugged. What were their chances for escape? None, he thought, the four men hemming them in tightly. They walked to a far off clearing barely visible in the thick orchard of lime trees. Maddalena nudged Chris and pointed to the makeshift tents in the distance. They stopped in front of the opening of the larger tent and the small soldier entered the tent to announce the capture to his commanding officer.

He emerged from the tent and shoved both of them inside where an officer sat behind a desk flanked by two orderlies. Chris breathed a sigh of relief. The officer was the veterinarian rebel Colonel who been friendly on the two occasions they met.

After standing at attention for several minutes, one of the orderlies shoved Chris forward to within arm's length of the

Colonel. He was smoking a thick cheroot and staring at the tent top.

Chris smiled and said, Buenos Dias, Senor."

The colonel craned his head to face Chris with a wan smile. "Buenos Dias." He placed his hands on the scarred table, held his head in his hands for an instant, and then, said in low voice, "It is not a fortunate day, Senor Scientist."

Chris clasped Maddalena close to his body, she was trembling. 'And I am not Senor Scientist. We are friends," said Chris cajoling.

"But that is not so today—this afternoon."

"What happened, we had such a rapport, intelligent conversations."

"We did indeed, but that was months ago. As change has occurred, which I personally regret, but there is such a thing as necessity, Senor."

"I am headed for the States." Chris stayed on point.

"We know, with Senorita Vasques. Need I ask you why?"

"I am homesick. I have been away too long. It is time I returned."

"And the Senorita, she is Mexican, no?"

"Colonel, am I a problem to the rebels. I thought you vetted me awhile back."

Not you, but the Senorita is." The Colonel nodded in Maddalena's direction.

Maddalena spoke up proudly, "My father was Antonio Vasquez!"

"Senorita Vasquez, you too are notable in our history, eh?" The colonel took a long drag on his cheroot, " History? History has become an artifact. No one remembers the grand revolution of Mexico, Zapata, Villa, today we have a movement a turmoil that is unrelated to the past, a mongrel of history."

A mongrel, I agree," said Chris trying to appear accommodating.

"But that is of no consequence this afternoon. None! I have a duty which I find disagreeable," the colonel's face darkened.

"Only hours to the border and we shall be out of Mexico and your concern." Chris sensed the sudden shift in his demeanor.

The colonel stood up and chucked his lit cheroot out the front of the tent opening. "I wish that were so. I wish I was back among my animals for this is foaling time. But I am here in this dismal tent with an unwelcome order on my desk."

Chris instinctively stepped in front of Maddalena and said, "You are free to do as you please."

"Would that it was so. The council has a long arm especially with traitors. They don't escape, that is a record and all Mexico knows it."

"If your orders are so disagreeable, then ignore them." Chris was in a panic at the word traitor.

"There is a squad outside that is witness to my duty. I would not have much life Senor if I were to fail. But that is not the point. Maddalena you were warned, you abused your father's reputation and the accommodation that provided."

"Colonel, what are you saying?" Chris wrapped his arms behind him to further shield Maddalena.

The colonel shuffled papers in front of him. "I have orders for her execution. Sorry."

"Allow me to plead for her life before the Council as she pleaded for mine." Chris wailed.

"They have dismissed you in their plans. You are a world celebrity of sorts. They don't need the publicity. Maddalena on the other hand is local and this is a local matter!"

"Then shoot me too!" Chris was frantic. Maddalena was limp behind him.

"Who said anything about shooting. Yes, yes, my first orders were to use a firing squad, but I made some changes. I prefer a more merciful end. Outside my tent in a thicket there is a makeshift hospital van, fully equipped. Maddalena will be led to the van, placed on a gurney and shot with massive doses of cocaine. This is my concession to a sad affair."

Chris lunged for the colonel but the orderlies intercepted him and restrained him. "I'll kill you first, you bastard!"

"Now, you must excuse me. I shall retire with a pipe of opium and try to forget this whole matter. You will be allowed to proceed on your way after you have witnessed the execution to your satisfaction."

A nod from the Colonel and the orderlies urged the fainting Maddalena and the struggling Chris out of the tent and in the direction of the van in the thicket. It was a converted army truck but well equipped with emergency machines. Two more orderlies awaited them and seized Maddalena at once. They placed her on a gurney and bound her with overlapping straps.

Maddalena reached out to Chris but he was restrained by three soldiers.

"Murder! Murder! Screeched Chris as the orderlies wound a rope around his neck to keep him quiet. A nurse appeared with a large syringe, efficiently tied a tourniquet to reveal a vein in Maddalena's right arm. They connect the syringe to the port and it began.

Chris tried to knock the syringe from the nurse's hands but the soldier stunned his shoulders with a blow of his rifle butt. Chris howled and crumpled to the floor.

Chris was forced to watch. When it was over he was bound and shoved out of the van into the nearby bushes. He vomited repeatedly and collapsed.

Coca Spirits

ours passed. Chris was in brambles and aggressive ants crawled over his body, covering his face and attacking his eyes. The rope around his neck tightened with movement, he could breathe in short gasps if the ants allowed him to open his mouth. The bramble hooked deeper as he moved. This misery was nothing compared to the despair of Maddalena's death.

He must have been unconscious for some time. He heard footsteps and an engine running, approaching. Two soldiers picked him up, unbound the bloody rope from his throat and pushed him towards his jeep standing by, motor running. He stumbled into the jeep. He glanced at the cargo area behind his seat and to his horror saw the outline of a body of in a native blanket. He let out a howl!

The soldier pressed him in to his seat and pointed his gun ordering him to move on.

Half delirious, Chris shifted gears and the jeep slowly moved out of the thicket to the open road. His eyes were blinded with tears that ran down his cheeks. Bleary eyed, the sunlight stung him. He drove for several miles and pulled over.

Was this a coca nightmare? The reality of the last forty eight hours flashed and surged back. Chris turned abruptly to the form behind him. Did they dare decapitate Maddalena as they had done with all their presumed traitors? Desecration of such order on Maddalena's body tempted him to blind his eyes forever. He groped behind to feel her, to find her head. The gruesomeness of her lifelessness took his breath. His fingers hesitantly felt through the covering blanket, then the tip, then a round object under his fingers. He moved it, it was intact. Maddalena was whole. He kissed his finger of contact and fainted.

Chris regained consciousness very slowly. He frantically tried to get his bearings. He was headed north, that he knew. He would follow this road to the border. He drove not too fast for fear of rocking the body behind him. It was a grueling trip and when he finally reached the crossing at Baja and when the border guards opened the driver's door he fell into a half unconscious swoon.

Chris could not form words. The guards edged him out of the seat and carried him to a patrol car. They drove him to a nearby headquarters, his jeep driven by another guard, followed them. He was delivered directly to an infirmary, where he was identified, bathed, treated for dehydration, deep bramble gouges, ant bites and the garroted neck wound. He collapsed and slept for days of hours.

When he awoke on the third day, there was hot coffee on the chest beside him, a military nurse and doctor at the foot of the bed discussing his condition. A sandwich was offered that he did not touch. The doctor nodded to a commander of the border patrol standing behind him.

"I think you can interview Dr. Christopherson, now, Commander. But please don't make it too long. He is still quite fragile.

Chris looked up at the tall figure next to his bed. The commander of the guard introduced himself and sat in a chair beside him.

"How are you doing, now, Dr. Christopherson?"

Chris had only one reply, "Maddalena!?"

"She has been taken to the morgue."

"The morgue?" Chris tried to focus.

"The heat, you know." The commander appeared sincere in his condolence.

Chris answered all questions as best he could. Then waved his hand to signal he could take no more.

After two more days of rest in the infirmary he was allowed to attend Maddalena's burial. The cemetery of a nearby convent had been selected, although disused for years, it was tucked away in the confines of a small garden with brief narrow headstones of dead nuns. It must have been a small order of Sisters. Chris had not been consulted about the burial, as it was expedited by Federal authorities. A priest was present to which Chris had no objection. When it was over, he was given a small wild rose from a wreath from the gravesite. He held it against his breast .

The following week Chris was met by a diplomatic attaché in charge of his return, now that he was on United States soil. He was given money on account, another passport and a plane ticket to Washington, D. C. Debriefing with various departments and assistants to the President awaited him. He did not want to leave her, he wished to remain longer to grieve. He was advised that the ticket was round trip and that he could return as he wished after his appointments.

Chris never returned. After his meeting with the Department of Defense, the Drug Enforcement Czar, and myriad global media, he suffered a complete nervous breakdown and was institutionalized at St. Elizabeth's Hospital for six months where he was treated for severe depression and anxiety.

Upon his release from St. Elizabeth's, Chris returned to the family ranch in Montana for further recuperation. His illness was reported widely and it took no time for his enemies to confirm that indeed he had probably been mentally ill for a very long time. They focused on his experience at the Bolivian telescope as a psychotic episode, that his vision and the appearance of the Cloud was the result of severe hallucinations, a cosmic mirage, a freakish atmospheric effect and the exhortations and warnings of the Cloud should be ignored. There would always be challenges, doubt and disbelief, but he was in no condition to defend anything. not now.

Preview

Chris sat in the cedar paneled library of the ranch house, internet screen by his side. He could see the wave of changes storming in the world. All cameras were focused on changes crucial to the demands of the Cloud. Clumsy steps forward, and better steps to follow. Not exactly an upheaval of the past errors and mismanagement, but a pubertal transformation that resembled a nascent world of the Cloud's intent. No formula, no ideology to guide the human race. When one thinks of it, would the only guiding force, the only dynamo, be love? Was it possible? At first, the intellectual Chris scoffed, love? Most love was self serving, mawkishness and insincerity. And yet the Cloud was power as it expressed itself purely. One had only to wait in prayer.

At times, the scenes on the screen mimicked a vast migration, a burgeoning of pilgrimages to war memorials, killing fields of battles, and unmarked graves asking for forgiveness and atonement. The civil atmosphere had changed. It reminded Chris of descriptions of the Middle Ages, the light was dimmer, sober like the beams on a napes under a Rose Window. That headlong speed of modernist man, at any cost of peace of mind or limb, was ebbing. A very restrained panic was pervasive. Muscles and hearts appeared ready for the race that could determine the fate of the humans. Politics and politicians moved swiftly like passenger birds alighting here, and then there. There was an enormous grinding, a change not for the sake of change but with a purpose. Like a monster glacier it was grinding all to a new mutability. Yet always, a devil who was ready to trip you and many resolves went haywire. No matter the evidence, there were people who would never believe. Only time would convince them. Chris was vigilant in his watch, a viewing of one day was unlike that of another, Chris thought. Changes moved like quixotic clouds.

There in the dark remote corners on his screen, he was reminded that he was under close surveillance, and the subject of a CIA study. There was, he guessed, always the possibility of an arrest for his use of cocaine, even within the prescribed and hereditary dose of the Incan mores. It was not yet legal. Perhaps the Cloud was wrong about coca. After all, they are children and believe it is something like soothe candy.

Chris was no longer on top of the world. No longer on the high altitude scopes that he called home since university days. He had been up to look up and now he was down to look down. How grand, it would be if he were flanked by Abigail Simpson and his Maddalena. Certainly, they would be a team to meet the exigencies of twenty years to come. Maddalena had been posthumously awarded the Pulitzer Prize as outstanding journalist. He was heartened. To him, at this level, it appeared that the modern world like a tram had hitched its suspenders to reach the Cloud's goals in the allotted time. Chris leaned back in his chair to relax his part until the mutation was over.

He endured attacks of insomnia when he thought there might be an anniversary day for the advent of the Cloud. He could not deny that there was a perpetual din in his ears, like the sound of a radio with volume off but the connection still humming. When the Cloud had passed over land it etherized a grace and caress, he thought.

His parents did not know what to make of their son, his physical and mental condition, the acclaim, his being chosen the interlocutor for the Cloud, the abuse, the celebrity? Their son, who as a boy insisted on being shepherd of a flock, to remain out all night under the stars and limitless horizon. They agreed that he was start struck from birth. The family rallied around him.

But no one addressed him again as scientist.

Court Martial

ashington was a stew of lawyers. A court martial of global interest was in session. Major General Darwin Learn, commander of the missile site deputed to fire on the asteroid 'Cloud' was being held accountable for lack of preparedness, dilatory wits before firing and general incompetence. He had been in full command of the elite unit of the US Army trained to safeguard the earth from extraterrestrial missile attack.

When not drunk with shame, he lamely burbled that a bird, a white raven confused the computer sighting and drew three launched missiles off course. He was asked sarcastically if it was the flutter of wings that confused the billion dollar equipment. The general took full responsibility for the mishap.

Some editorials were solemn about the explanation, stranger things were happening, given the appearance of the Cloud. There was opinion that perhaps a flock of Canadian geese impeded the sighting and in columnar flight appeared as one huge bird.

But the General declared repeatedly that he saw a normal sized raven. Much to his dishonor no ornithologist had ever recorded the sighting of a white raven and that scientific community ridiculed the whole affair. 'Were we slipping into a lexicon of mythology,' they taunted. His peers quipped 'whatever did the General drink the night before at the Officers Club?'

The court martial was a closed hearing, shining in brass upper ranks, no animal presence. Was the animal tribunal aware of this other trial bearing on the Cloud? Were they kept informed? There was much speculation.

Chris had been subpoenaed to testify in the trial. As he walked from his hotel to the Court this autumn morning, his eyes turned skyward. Not an unusual occurrence and he was always more comfortable there. But it was not the sky that caught his attention, but a noisy flock of at least one hundred starlings appeared to follow his every step. They hovered as he ascended the steps to the Military Court.

There was much technical testimony to wade through before they finally called Chris to the stand in the late afternoon. He stated for the record that he had no knowledge of a white raven and could not comment on the fact that General Learn's missiles had failed to hit the target. No, there was no additional communication from the Cloud that would shed light on the aberration.

The Pentagon was embarrassed and the tribunal officers grimaced as they presided. If the notes of this hearing were made public it would be a porridge no one could digest. This was not their cup of tea so they side stepped into the wings of this staged process to order a special congressional commission to investigate further the allegations of the General, and other aspects of the disturbance that from the onset, the Cloud was creating.

All kidding aside, the threat of the Cloud could not be ignored. The only way to address this bizarre defense by the General was to engage a select panel of professional ornithologists for a rational explanation or denial.

All that was contained in the record of the military tribunal was translated in human and animal language throughout the world. While the court martial was in process it was noted globally that whales did not click, apes did not chatter, birds did not sing, lions, did not roar, elephants did not trumpet, frogs did not croak, falcons did not scream, snails stopped hissing, donkeys did not bray, dophins did not splash, ducks did not quack, all tongues subdued. What the animal court thought of the process the starlings did not tell! .

In testifying before the congressional committee given the task of investigation, thirty experts agreed, 'No, clearly there is no record of a white raven in existence. It the far reaches of possibility there could be one that flew off course from a remote tropical region where most exotic birds are bred. They knew they were at the limits of their scientific realities but under oath they could not deny this far flung explanation and at this point ever since the appearance of the Cloud anything was possible, wasn't it? The most remote reaches of the Amazon were the most rational locale, they opined.

The chairman of the congressional committee felt most comfortable passing this porcupine once more. How the hell did he end up with this on his plate? And in an election year?

The committee commissioned an expedition to consist of Audubon Society specialists supported by military and governmental escort to search for this white raven. The focus of their search as directed by the ornithologists would be the remote Amazon as far as the Pacific, if needed. They insisted that Dr. Christopherson accompany the expedition as there was tacit agreement among the congressman that Chris knew more than he was saying.

The Expedition

~☁~

T he expedition force was given two weeks to prepare. Chris had returned to the ranch for a respite, but readied himself nonetheless.

The New York Times assigned a reporter to travel with the group and report on the progress of the bird hunt. Prior to the launch of the expedition he reported that the effect of the congressional committee directive was that thousands upon thousands of bird watchers roamed any nearby forest and glen for a sign of a white raven. Public parks were being trampled by the hordes toting scopes, tripods, and video equipment. Cults were arising in minority ghettoes who were wearing scapulas with the image of the white raven. People with a singular focus merged in mob hysteria, a rage, a fashion, a new icon to replace all medals. Close behind was an outpouring of songs that hit gold record rewards. Jewelers were not far behind with their jeweled representations. The pornographers had a ball, seeing the raven as enemy they did all to create obscene hilarity and discredit.

From Andrews Air Force Base, the Army Transport, carrying a team of thirty, took off for Rio de Janiero with a connecting flight via smaller aircraft to Manaus, the jump off point on the expedition's Amazon journey.

The two riverboats were loaded with field apparatus of bird artists, easel, paints, sighting scopes, and a deck full of the most sophisticated digital and video cameras as well as two months of provisions. Aboard was the Minister of the Brazilian Amazon, an interior department attache, two Ecuadoran zoologists, a US Army special forces team, six ornithologists, Chris, two interpreters, two river guides, a maintenance crew of four, the New York Times journalist and a correspondent for the BBC.

If Chris had had any objection to the trip they phased out as he hailed a grand view of the opening of the Amazon. The swift steamboats broached the rain forests in the long trip westward, guided by dolphins forever hoping to reach the Pacific at the other end. Dipping and soaring familiarly with long snouts, they cooled the heated boredom. This thousand mile trip into the jungles gave you an idea of the sportsmanship of the Audubon group. Half of the party convinced of the existence of the white raven, and half in good humored disbelief.

The river boats made several landfalls, cautiously winding through tributaries under watchful eyes from behind the jungle. Throughout the weeks there was no cloud cover, the jungle growth overhung the river so you steamed under an umbrella of rare trees. Never had Chris experienced such a blossoming of flowers. It was as if he was in an orchidaceous hothouse.

After a month's time they arrived at their prime destination, the lands occupied by the Jivaro Indians. Chris was warned what to expect when they landed at the dock.

A decorated and painted Shaman greeted them, flanked by the Tribal Chief and ten warriors. The interpreter stepped onto the dock warily as the Jivaro were known to always antagonistic to the visit of westerners.

The Minister stepped forward. He had been elected as their spokesman. His prior intelligence had indicated that the Jivaro were currently at war with two tribes, they had decimated one and now in the process of killing off the others, and shrinking their heads as trophy. Historically, no war was ever declared, but they were notorious for their genocidal raids.

The first question was answered quickly. 'No, they had never seen a white raven,' then the Shaman with ridiculous smile asked if they would like to buy parrots or parrot feathers, instead. The minister explained through the interpreter that they were of singular purpose on this expedition and he requested their permission to comb the Jivaro territory on their own in search of this elusive bird with guarantees that they would disturb nothing and not interefere with them.

The Shaman shared this information with the Tribal Chief and his guard. The leader shook his head negatively. He stared at the two boats.

"Of course, we bring gifts and supplies for the tribe and bolts of cloth much desired by the women." The interpreter pointed to the stores on the deck of his steamboat.

The tribal chief softened his attitude. After much parlay back and forth he finally agreed to allow the expedition two weeks on his land to search and film this never seen bird.

"A search for a white raven? The Chief shook his head, and pulled a white feather from the necklace of a nearby guard, and sneered.

The Minister had consented to join the expedition because Brasilia wanted an in person assessment of the reported recent aggressions of the Jivaros on the tribe to their North. Scouts reported two thousand were slain, beheaded and cannibalized in their most recent raid. He had not ventured into the tributaries in years discouraged by the unchanging feral tribes of the region, of which the Jivaros were the worst. They were notorious and had an incorrigible taste for blood. The Jivaro were the largest exporters of tropical birds in the world and that is why they had come here. Was this the most likely place for a white raven to appear? He had agreed to keep an eye on this expedition sensation for his government, but the white raven was second place in his thoughts.

The Jivaros were shrewd traders and knew their market. Shrunken desiccated heads of the enemy decorated the living rooms of the Brazilian demi monde. Even though they had contact for many years they adopted no western customs or politics and managed a Spanish lingo, probably for business purposes. The tribal chief and the Shaman ruled the roost on the basis of savage power. Possessors of a large region of Amazon basin, they were forty thousand strong. The Minister knew they were masters with no obligations to the Brazilian government.

Were the Jivaro less than a model for a sovereign world? The minister asked himself when he reviewed dispatches from Europe, the Middle East, Africa and Latin America. If they clamped down on the Jivaro what example could he cite in his world to prove that one mode of living was better than another.

He began to doubt the entire mission and referred to it sarcastically as a fool errand. He blamed Chris with sidelong glances. The scientists had deferred to Chris from natural courtesy and professional pride, but they all thought there was something wrong with him, as if he had been dipped into a batter and emerged as something else.

The ornithologists conferenced secretly, would Chris be the first man to spy the white raven with the accruing honors. Did his relationship to the Cloud give him advantage? Chris chose to remain on the sidelines and kept a low profile.

About the end of the second week, the ornithologists and photographers had had their fill of birds of all kinds but no white raven.

A young warrior was sent by the Shaman on the fifteenth morning. He advised them through the interpreter that they had overstayed their welcome and that they must make plans to leave.

They needed to return to the affairs of their tribe and that the Shaman sensed that the expedition had been bad medicine.

It was time to go, they all agreed. The search had been exhaustive and they were running out of supply. They promised to depart in two days time as it would take that long to retrieve all equipment and members of the teams deployed in the jungle.

It was just after dawn when a large company of Jivaro warriors led by the Shaman and Chief gathered at the dock to bid them farewell. Before the Shaman began the interpreter interrupted to say that the Minister had one more mission to complete.

The Minister stepped forward and began to explain that three years ago a mysterious sky object, thought to be a dangerous asteroid in orbit around the earth had been discovered by Dr. Christopherson while doing deep sky research in Australia. He explained that Chris had tracked and traced its motion in the heavens for three years because its behavior was very odd and erratic, unlike anything heretofore observed. It was believed that this asteroid like object if on the right path could easily annihilate earth and everything on it. Ultimately this sky object approached Earth in the form of a massive Cloud and hovered for days. He explained further that is deputized Dr. Christopherson, who he pointed to, as its spokesman, its shaman of sorts.

The Shaman stared at Christopher not fully understanding the Minister's point, yet.

"Within a short time, this Cloud let itself be known," he continued, "announcing that it was made up of the unborn aborted children of earth. It did indeed threaten to annihilate man if the human race could not heal itself." He referenced the tribunal and the sentencing of man. He then went on to describe the edicts of the Cloud as best he could in translation, ending with the term of twenty years provided for compliance, a probationary period in which to reform and changeover into a world worthy of man. He warned the Jivaro Chief that he, his tribe and his whole life style was in total opposition to the edicts and that he should repent and change, now before it was too late. The minister stepped back, satisfied that he had found a way to deal with the Jivaro after all. There would be accolades at the Capital, he thought.

At the end of the Minister's communication, the Shaman laughed and held his paunch, green spittle on his lips. He said in a voice hurled at Chris in a shriek.

"Ah, you monsters! You come here with the excuse of a search for this white raven! Instead, as you have done in the past you intent to get rid of us, by means of our own suicide. If I was to explain to the warriors here, what you intend to do to the tribe, they will kill you where you stand. Whatever this devil is, he is in collusion with you to eliminate us by any means, this time by trickery and not useless force of arms." He exhaled in a great burst of air as if preparing to spit.

"We defy you in the face of these threats. They are lies! Extinction! We have been threatened with extinction for a thousand years. Your soldiers came to conquer us to make us slaves, and you did not succeed. Many of your bravest sit on the shelves of my log house, heads grinning. We have faced drought, floods, quakes of the earth and we have prevailed.

The tribal chief moved forward to confront the Minister. "We have fended off the attacks of nearby tribes, the exploitation of traders and dealers dishonest as snakes and now we deal on equal terms. This lie of your power to monitor us is a fiction of your government, an attempt to remake the Jivaro nation into plantation slaves. You do not understand our way. They would lose heart and die by the thousands in the slums of your cities. Sir, as you value your life and the life of the crew, do not make these demands and mention threats of extinction. We agreed with courtesy to allow you to search our forests. Your gifts will be returned in order to protect us from the evil spirit they carry to us. They are cursed objects." The Chief retreated into the protection of his guard.

The Shaman shouted at top voice, "We were the plumes of an eagle, not your white raven!" This phrase he said with contempt. "In response, we shall have a week's festivites of forty thousand Jivaros to prove our survival for the future. You will remain but you will not be invited because your bad medicine must be destroyed. We will feast as never before and crown the honor of the Jivaro tribe! Watch us dance and feast, jousting that you will envy," he roared at them.

"White raven, indeed! You will report back to the world that we do not honor this 'Cloud' you talk of." He broke a spear in his hands. "In the meantime you be will our prisoners until after the feast and we decide what to do with you all!"

Fear struck the crew with a sudden gust from the Pacific. The river guide arose and spoke. "My men are innocent natives of the Amazon. We know of no plot. Spare us from your revenge. We don't care what happens to your enemies!"

The Jivaro nation feasted for five days. Dressed in finest war paint and trophies, they displayed all the decadence they promised. They raided wantonly, cannibalized, killed with savagery as never before. They danced in wild reverie taunting the Cloud to rain on them.

In one week's time, the nation of the Jivaro, a territory as large as the state of Montana had been devastated, animal and plant. The calamity as witnessed by Chris and the crew was like a scything hurricane that leveled all things in its path. The bird population centuries old fled somewhere, not a fledgling could be found.

The Shaman appeared in person demanding an audience with Chris. He was surrounded by warriors bedraggled and moaning misery. The Shaman was evidently in the grip of drugs, he floundered on his feet, knelt and rotated himself. All the while green spittle stained his chin when he spoke,this time in perfect Spanish. He had been to Seminary in his youth.

The crew begged Chris to meet the Shaman figuring it their only hope. The Shaman approached and knelt at Chris' feet. He mumbled almost incoherently, "Help us. The power is real, it exists, whatever it is, and surely it must be a devil. The children are dying, nothing is born,." he pleaded.

Chris spoke, "Like you we are also under the power of the Cloud. I, we can promise nothing. We shall wait and see what happens in the next few days. Your repentance may return the sun, let the foaling begin and the birds return." He was very uncomfortable in the desperate position of prophet.

The Shaman squirmed on the ground, then, assumed what appeared to be the form of a crocodile. The native crew said that he was a powerful shaman and was now indeed a crocodile of the River. But they could give no reason for the Shaman to assume an animal form at this juncture.

Suddenly, it began to rain, at first merficully, warm rain and mild mist, then steadier, the trees began to sway, green tendrils sprouted from the parched earth.

The power had kept its word.

The dramatic change in the lives of the Jivaro Indians was a worldwide headline. The BBC declared that their correspondent had indeed witnessed the power and promise of the Cloud in person. A sovereign nation, guilty as the Jivaro had been of the most heinous crimes of man had mutated under the gavel of the Cloud and in turn the Cloud had shown love and mercy and redemption.

The New York Times journalist was quoted as saying that 'it was no longer necessary to prove that celestial interference, the white raven, derailed the missile firings.' And yet, as he half expected, this reality was strangely received with subdued mood. In their hearts most humans wished that the Cloud had never appeared and the nations could go on in their historical trail of mayhem.

Chris made no public statement. As a willing go between he awaited the voice of the children and took no privileges.

Summa

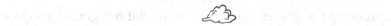

S o Chris passed the years on the Montana ranch with his aging and dying parents, but with a new hum in his heart. While others seized the limelight in the corrected culture and politics, he was forgotten. He was professionally denied a scope on any mountain or desert so his naked eye sought the Cloud behind the moon.

His daily ration of cocaine gave him vigor and with every dose he thought of Mexico, Bolivia, rebels, Federales, Abigail Simpson and Maddalena. He had Maddalena's remains placed in his family graveyard. He would someday lie beside her under a manna moon.

A miracle? No! Chris did not believe so. Even twenty years was not enough time to erase the infamies of a long, long, past, but he witnessed vast improvements. He hailed the abrogation of genocide, moral wars and the elimination of abortion, pornography and institutional killing. Freedom of religion increased. Importantly, there was an increase in representational elections of a people's democracy and restraints on private wealth and banking.

The air appeared cleaner and fresher, cleansed, less bloodstained earth and man closer in space.

Chris could see with naked eye that the Cloud was serene where it was hugging the moon mother.

Under a silvery pine lay the body of Maddalena. Years back his family got permission to install a burial plot on part of their immense acreage. Family and dear friends used the same lot with similar leaded names on markets. A gathering of herders at nightfall appeared to candle the plot. The rolling grazing ground of the Christopherson family was a vast as the starry sky. A palisade enclosed the plot to keep out coyotes, wolves or badgers from uprooting the graves. Sheep and goats did not graze this close.

Chris in quiet moments near her grave, asked why it took so long for him to fall in love? From the beginning of his life he stubbornly thought that his life was a trial of self development, a kind of praxis that would fully involve all the steps of his term. And yet, he was thirty eight when he loved Maddalena. What had displaced all those necessities for what we call fulfillment. Was his absorption in the sky a lack of vitality? Or perhaps the cause was the lengthy pause for a four flagstone leap?

The Cloud? Now in his middle fifties he loved skyward. No grip of a scope, the explosive light of a stellar nova. What was meaningful and satisfied his restless soul was a prophetic aura that would expiate his guest.

Did the Cloud feel it? Did he wish it? That Maddalena's love was inclusive. Love, this is what the Cloud asked of humans, to accept the capacity to love in the highest and allow it to guide all morality? All liveliness? The poignancy of love, the rewards of the word were so true, so beautiful. Chris' double star was in an orbit of love. Chris reflected that a global change of heart of this magnitude could only happen if there had been a massive intrusion of love. Was it a moon exerting a tidal wave of love? But these questions were moot when one witnessed the changes in living together in the new order of human kind.

On a visit, one would expect to see a hobby observatory on the highest peak of the ranch lands but there was none. Chris explained that his eyes were failing, and he felt that peering in the skies after his experience of the Cloud was an intrusion, as if peeking into someone's living room.

He sat in his father's warn leather recliner in the library staring out of the double picture window and wondered if he would live it out. Those probationary twenty years.

Valentines

Today was the judgment anniversary of the appearance of the Cloud. The world was waiting for its reprieve and the imprimatur. The world thought it had complied with the edicts. However, it if the Cloud did not return, was all of this sacrifice a joke, a japery in the sky? Tension everywhere was tight and nervous. It was a mixing bowl of belief and convictions and controversy and its eventual import. Beaters were whirling and melding and separating, kneading again into various mixtures and products. A dough with new thought and old theories, gewgaws flew apart by the vortex of the changes. A grinding of mania and deep introspection was at the bottom of the bowl.

In these twenty years, the experience of the Cloud had become a somewhat hazy legend in the minds of the populace and a fable of sorts to the new generation. In the hands of scalawags, the asteroid was the butt of a joke, sometimes even scatological. Some distinctions and uniqueness of the Cloud was a blurred aegis and exaggeration.

Chris realized this and knew it was necessary for him, a conscientious duty, to keep alive the lucidity and matchless beauty of the experience.

In anticipation of the anniversary, an oratorio of sorts was written for animals. A variety of animals were arranged on the stage of Carnegie Hall in New York City. They were accompanied by dissonant chords by the composer. The animals brayed, cawed, roared , growled, caterwauled, chirped, croaked, howled, hissed in a chorale. The audience was pleased but confounded and saw in the stage the historic image of the tribunal of the Cloud.

Animal shelters became numerous and refined to the point of comfort, horses groomed with loving care, the zoos received grants and benefices beyond use. A boom for ignored creatures, it was an animal Eden.

A flock of birds were singing in the grasslands surrounding the veranda upsetting Chris' bursts of dozing. Flocks of yellow canaries with gold tipped wing feathers soared above his head, making sure to waken him.

With the near speed of light a rose colored canopy covered the earth, pulsating evenly. A catching optimism imbued the air. The canaries sang breathlessly. All humans tuned to a mesmeric silence. Would Chris be called upon to break the silence, to recite the judgment? A balm in the air. Forests stretched upward to touch the rim of the canopy. Sprouts cleared the soil, lambs frolic in the high meadow. Happy chattering from all throats.

'The Judgement, the judgement? That was the inarticulate cry from silent hearts.

Stars were stage struck.

Chris was not needed to speak for the Cloud. The children in the Cloud spoke not loudly, but symbolically.

The rain! No rain. The air shimmered with bursts of pyrotechnical glows of lightning bolts, harmless without thunder. A display of exoneration and victory. But that was not all. The rain, the rain of love notes from the unborn children addressed to all. From all quarters of the globe fell paper-like squares by the billions, like snowflakes in a dense blizzard.

The sheep dogs at Chris' feet howled in surprise.

What, something to read? Short poems in scribbled hand read in all languages:

Robins are nice
And twice
We love you!

There was no monogram, no signature from the Cloud. A poem addressed to each.
Pansies in a row
Bright faces up
Promise you
A better day!

For Maddalena, he read with tears.
Lilies are white
The heart is red
I love you.
A song is sung
I am here
A listening leaf

A shower of Valentines! Chris' body stiffened with pride, a bloodstream of certainty. Above his head was a double star of silver streaks.
A frosted dome arose, a rotunda, an opening to the sky, a round of children's faces, childish voices, No longer a wonder, but a matter of fact.
Then all vanished. The earth appeared usual, and night fell with an amalgam of sunsets.
Christopher sat unmoved in his chair facing the humpbacked hills, its deepening blue darkness, the double star fading.
A white raven perched on his arm.